RECAPTURING Youth

ADVENTURES OF A VIRGIN BACKPACKER

JOHN B MCMILLAN

Copyright © 2022 by John B McMillan

Paperback: 978-1-958381-36-6
eBook: 978-1-958381-37-3
Library of Congress Control Number: 2022913915

All rights reserved. No part of this publication may be reproduced, distributed, or transmitted in any form or by any electronic or mechanical means, without the prior written permission of the publisher, except in the case of brief quotations embodied in critical reviews and certain other noncommercial uses permitted by copyright law.

This is a work of nonfiction.

Table of Contents

Introduction

*Youth would be an ideal state if it came
later in life: Lord Asquith, 1923.*

The sound of ice grinding against the hull of the ship penetrated the drowsiness of an ebbing tide of sleep. I checked my watch: 6 a.m. - time for another snooze before breakfast. But first, I reached up and drew the curtain aside from the porthole: ice, everywhere. Large ice floes growled alongside as the ship thrust her way through a soup of brash-ice, glacial debris like the aftermath of a gigantic explosion, which covered the surface of the sea between ship and shore. It was an inhospitable coastline: no beaches, no landing places. Black mountains rose steeply from the sea. Along their ridges, deep snow had been sculpted into delicately patterned cornices by the wind. Glaciers, like giant textured brushstrokes, painted the valleys between the peaks.

Snug in the warmth of my blankets I felt a glow - like an inward smile. Here at last. Funny how so many long-held dreams had come to pass, I reflected: exploring the sun-kissed islands of the South Pacific, the enigma that is Easter Island, diving on the Great Barrier Reef, trekking in the Andes, and the ultimate destination - Antarctica. It has often been said to me, "How lucky you are. You have the perfect lifestyle."

Lucky? Maybe… Maybe not.

It's strange how the most seemingly innocuous events can become the significant waypoints of life. My mind drifted back several years to a Saturday morning when, intending to spend some time in the garden, I was taken aback when Katie, my wife, asked me to come shopping with her. This was not something we enjoyed sharing. For me, shopping is the very antithesis of enjoyment.

Seeing the look on my face, she pleaded with me. "Please. You can go to the bookshop while I do my bit. I just want you to do the driving and for company. We'll have lunch somewhere."

Something in her voice compelled me to resist the temptation to argue. I couldn't refuse, though it did puzzle me a bit.

Browsing in the bookshop, my attention was attracted by a title: 'Undertaken With Love - The Story of a DIY Funeral.' The idea of a Do It Yourself funeral appealed to me. I bought the book. It described a woman's efforts to have her husband disposed of as he had wished: no undertakers, just a few close friends and family, and his ashes to be dug into the garden. His unconventional wishes caused difficulties for his wife who had to overcome many obstacles; notably a lack of cooperation from the undertaking profession when it came to procuring a coffin. I found it absorbing. Later that night, I put my book down and turned to Katie.

"Maybe it's about time we made plans for our funerals. The boys should know in case we both go at the same time if, for example, we were both killed in a road accident. Have you any thoughts about how you would like to be disposed of when your time comes?"

She came out with a straight answer.

"I don't see the sense in having an expensive funeral. I don't want any money wasted on flowers. You have tools and a shed to work in, so you can make me a box, put me in the back of the Volvo, and the boys can help you carry me. There's no need to hire a hearse when there's a car perfectly capable of doing the job sitting at the door - and I don't want any miserable looking strangers in black coats and top hats!"

She was right of course. The Volvo estate car could accommodate a coffin quite easily. I laughed. "That'll certainly get folk talking."

"It won't bother me. But I'm telling you now I don't want money wasted on an expensive funeral. I would rather see the money go to a good cause - like the Highland Hospice."

"I've no argument against that."

"Fine, you can get busy anytime you like and get the coffins made while you're still fit, and let the boys know what we want done."

This very pragmatic approach to funeral arrangements by an unpretentious lady came as no surprise to me. I had been married to her for almost thirty years, courted her for three years before that and, as a dutiful husband who always did as he was told, I saw no reason to change the habits of a lifetime. It never struck me as odd that she should expect the Volvo still to be around when she died - but they do seem to last forever.

Considering that we disagreed on just about everything else in life, it was a relief that we could agree on this. Well, that's not quite accurate. The notable exceptions were the really important things: bringing up children, the care of our dogs, and the sanctity of our marriage. Apart from these three we had disagreed on just about everything else. It was nice to find a fourth thing we could agree upon.

There's nothing original about the idea of a DIY funeral. You only need to go back a few generations to find that, in many rural areas at least, it was the norm rather than the exception. In many societies in other parts of the world it would be unthinkable to hand over the preparations for the disposal of the dead to anyone outside the family.

I laughed at the thought of a pair of coffins lying about the house. "Still, I suppose we could use them for storing the bedding until we need them." On the Monday morning I was back at work and forgot the matter.

I didn't know it then, but my wife was dying of cancer.

It was back in 1964 that I had vowed to care for Katie, 'In sickness and in health till death do us part.' That had never been a difficult promise to carry out. Apart from the two pregnancies, she had only consulted a doctor once in the thirty-three years I had known her.

The true meaning of our marriage vows was finally realised in April 1994, almost a year after our conversation, when she was diagnosed as suffering from an incurable cancer. We knew the cancer would win the physical battle, but we were determined it would never defeat our spirits.

Four months later she was dead.

I made her a coffin, and we had a DIY funeral. The reaction of friends and family was interesting, with comments ranging from, "Oh, no! Don't you know you can get counselling?" to "That is inspiring. I wish more people had the courage to do that." After the memorial service in the church, our two boys and myself - just the three of us, as per her wishes - carried her coffin from the church to the Volvo. I had made a special cradle to make this possible. It had a symbolism that appealed to me. The two boys held it on each side at the front; I took the rear, with the body of the woman who had brought us together between us. A single red rose from our garden was all that adorned her coffin. The funeral costs amounted to only £94, but along with generous donations from mourners who packed the church, we donated the cost of a commercial funeral to the Highland Hospice, where she died, and Macmillan Cancer Relief, in appreciation of the superlative care bestowed by their nurses.

My wife had never been keen on travel. I had envisaged life in retirement as a chain of endless days pottering in the garden. But now, the large garden where we had spent so much time together had become a burden. It was laden with memories of our life together, and part of me seemed to have died with Katie. It is difficult to describe the void left behind by death. We had ceased to be two separate people. We had become a couple - and one half of that was missing.

My response to stress had always been to keep busy so that I wouldn't have time to dwell on things. Always active in the community, I found I was now so busy that I had no time left for myself. No time to do what I wanted to do, rather than what was expected of me - no time to grieve, even. I suffered from exhaustion and bouts of depression. I felt like a ship without a compass, lost in a fog - and my self-esteem plummeted.

I remembered her words to me as she lay dying, "Make the most of every day." Both my sons were married, so I only had myself to look after. I retired and moved to a cottage on the west coast, severing my ties with the community I had served as head of the secondary school for 15 years. It was time to create a new life.

My love of sailing among the islands of Scotland's west coast would continue to satisfy my lust for adventure in summer, but I wanted to exchange the damp chill of the Scottish winter for something exotic. Package holidays and cruise ships do not excite me. I wanted to travel independently, explore far-off places, become acquainted with the people and their cultures. I did some sums: I could go a long way on what I could save on heating, lighting, telephone, food and car expenses. Sleeping in budget accommodation - youth hostels and the like - I could travel for months on end. Mixing with people from different parts of the world, I would never be lonely. I bought a cheap Round The World air ticket and went to the army surplus store to buy a rucksack.

"Where are you planning on going?" asked the shop assistant.

"Around the world," I said.

"But that's only a weekend pack!"

"I'm going to the tropics. I'll travel light."

Casting off the shackles of life as a retired headmaster, I set off to seek adventure. Life would never be the same again.

Many of the young people I met had told me they were travelling, "To find myself." I was a bit sceptical of that notion. Now I'm beginning to wonder. My aim in travelling had been to observe and experience other cultures, but travel has the power of revelation, and I had also been compelled to see *myself* through the eyes of others. My naivety and innocence defined me as a virgin backpacker, with a trail of blunders and confusion littering my pathway around the world. Yet it proved to be an amusing, cathartic, and rejuvenating experience.

Retirement is not an end. It can be the beginning of a new way of life, rich in opportunity for recapturing at least some of the vigour of youth. And, with the advantage of a lifetime's experience, we may well find that youth *is* an ideal state when it comes later in life.

Chapter 1

SPOILT FOR CHOICE

"Two eggs over easy with hash and a double latte no sugar with toasted rye and low fat non cholesterol vegetable oil spread on the side and no preserves."

I gazed in stunned amazement as my host, Marilyn, spat out her order for breakfast, the words rattling out like a machine gun. And I thought we spoke the same language! Even more amazingly, the waitress understood all this gobbledygook and noted the order without a hint of hesitation. I had to have 'eggs over easy' explained to me. That's how ignorant I was. I didn't want to reveal my ignorance further by asking for a translation of all the rest. I just stayed ignorant.

The American way of life is beyond my comprehension. Their kitchens must be the most expensively equipped parts of their homes, yet rarely get used for making much more than a cup of coffee. When pangs of hunger strike, they're more likely to jump in the car and head for the local diner rather than stroll into the kitchen and rustle up an omelette. Marilyn had insisted that I savour this aspect of American culture and took me out for breakfast.

Out for breakfast? In Scotland, I sup my porridge at home; still half asleep, hair tousled and eyes half-closed. But here I was, seated in what looked like a railway dining car, a fugitive from the despondent gloom of an imminent Scottish winter. I was on my way to Tahiti to spend a few months exploring the islands of the South Pacific, but London to Tahiti is a long haul (it's even longer from Lochcarron, Scotland), so I had included a stopover in the USA for a few days to visit Marilyn and Alex, a couple of school friends I hadn't seen for thirty-six years. This would also allow me to see the fabled glories of New England in the Fall and observe the behaviour of *Homo Sapiens Americanis* in his native habitat. It was an interesting diversion.

I studied the menu with little understanding and looked around in amazement at the enormous plates heaped with food being consumed by the other patrons. It's little wonder they have an outsize obesity problem here. The waitress looked at me expectantly.

I recognised the word 'oatmeal' on the menu and made a guess that this meant porridge and asked for some with a cup of tea. Very Scottish. Nice and simple, I thought. Huh. Nothing is that simple. In the USA you gotta have choices!

"What kinda tea d'ya like?" spat out the waitress through her chewing gum, with the characteristic staccato accent of north-eastern USA. "Indian, Chinese, green, iced, herbal, camomile, lavender, raspberry….?"

"Have ye no' got just an ordinary cup of tea? You know, the kind you make with a tea bag?" I pleaded.

"You mean regular tea?" Her surprised attitude suggested that asking for regular tea must be most irregular.

"Is that the kind that comes hot, with a dark brown colour, and you put milk and sugar in it?"

"Yeah. Like English breakfast tea?" That sounded promising.

"Aye, that'll do me fine." I was relieved that I was getting somewhere at last.

"D'ya like milk?" She fired back rapidly. "Full cream, half cream, skimmed, semi-skimmed, soya milk, coconut milk, goat's milk, yak's milk, camel's milk…"

"Cow's milk, full cream," I interrupted before she named every animal with a mammary gland that had escaped the flood and booked a berth on Noah's Ark. I was getting the hang of this game now, I thought. Maybe I could beat her at her own game and added, "From a Jersey cow, fed only on grass, not silage, and drawn by the hand of an eighteen year-old virgin with golden hair tied in pigtails, from the rear, left teat on the udder of the fourth cow on the north side of the milking parlour, pasteurised, homogenised and chilled to exactly a temperature of four degrees Celsius – please."

It costs nothing to be polite after all and my mother had always insisted on good manners. I sat back smugly. My smugness evaporated under another barrage of choices.

"D'ya like sugar? White, brown, demerara, honey, syrup, or saccharin."

"White, please."

"D'ya want toast?"

"Yes, please."

"Whitewholemealorrye?"

"Pardon?"

She repeated and I was still none the wiser. I gaped pleadingly at Marilyn, who translated, "White bread, wholemeal bread or rye bread." By now I was not only exasperated, I was feeling stupid as well.

"Wholemeal," I muttered.

"Butter, margarine, low fat, unsaturated easy spread low cholesterol vegetable oil...."

"Butter," I spat out.

"Is that regular butter or peanut butter?"

"Regular!" My voice raised a decibel or two.

"D'ya like marmalade, jam, honey, marmite, vegemite....."

"Marmalade!" I roared at her.

"Orange, lemon, or lime?" I groaned. I knew she had me beaten.

"Orange," I replied meekly, "And can I please have my breakfast now? I'm hungry." That seemed to appeal to her softer side.

"Sure. Where d'ya come from? Y'aint from around these parts. I can tell." Did it show that much? Maybe she had a brain after all. I decided to play the question game.

"Where do you think I come from?"

"Canadian?" I shook my head.

"English?"

"Try again."

"Irish?"

"You're getting closer."

"Hey, I got it. You're Scottish, right?"

"Aye, how did you guess?"

"You sound just like Sean Connery."

"Do you like Sean Connery?"

"Do I *like* Sean Connery?" Her eyes rolled heavenwards and then glazed over. She was on a flight path to orgasm. I titillated her further.

"Would you like to serve Sean Connery breakfast?"

"Would I like to serve Sean Connery breakfast?" Was this woman programmed only to ask questions? She savoured the thought for a moment, fantasising over a pre-breakfast romp with Mr Connery.

"Ooooh yeeeaaaah!" She had her orgasm at last.

"Well in that case would you mind serving *me* breakfast before you feel another orgasm coming on, or you'll have a death due to starvation on your conscience." That broke her fantasy. She became the professional waitress again.

"Anything else ya'd like?"

I flickered my eyebrows mischievously at her. "Mmmm. I wouldn't mind some of what you'd like to give Sean Connery."

Her eyes flashed and she almost blushed. Then she smiled at Marilyn, flicked her eyes towards me and said, "He's kinda cute, aint he? I love that Scotch accent."

At last, she marched off to get my porridge, happily fantasising about her pre-breakfast romp with Mr Connery and what sexy negligee she would wear. I have no doubt she would have a choice: Black, red, white, pink...?

Chapter 2

STUMBLING WITH STATISTICS

Having finished breakfast, we went off to look at the trees. I expected to be able to go wandering happily through woods carpeted with fallen leaves and glowing with autumn tints. If you go further inland into the mountain areas you can do just that, but there aren't many opportunities in the hundred-mile strip between Hartford and Boston. There is the occasional designated park with well-defined tracks to wander along. But mostly it's a leafy suburbia, interspersed at intervals of fifteen minutes driving time, with almost identical civic centres comprising shopping malls surrounded by acres of tarmac with parking lots, petrol stations, used car lots, and the ubiquitous McDonald's burger joints. You can go to sleep in the passenger seat of a car and wake up an hour later and you would swear that you were in the same place.

Standing out in stark contrast to all this and the brilliant red and yellow hues of the surrounding trees are white-painted New England style churches from the 19th or early 20th century with elegant, slender spires. That I liked. Picturesque. It was a pity about the architectural heritage of the late twentieth century.

New England in the Fall

Autumn colour attracts thousands of tourists to New England. The daily weather bulletins on radio and TV even tell you what percentage of the leaves have changed colour in each district so you can pick the best bits to see: "Oak County leads the field today with 88% colour just ahead of Ash County with 85%," chirps the announcer with a dazzling smile. They always sound excited, and I hate them for their perfectly manicured teeth.

That made me think. How do you estimate how many of the billions of leaves on millions of trees have changed colour? Do they have teams of people going out every day to count the red, yellow and green leaves? How do they stay awake? I suppose they must use satellite pictures; but fancy going to all that trouble just to count leaves.

It's the American way. They gotta have statistics. Watch any game of American football, a great misnomer if ever there was one, for the only time ball and foot make contact is when they stop the game to allow a player to try to kick it over the goals - maybe only two or three times per match.

Most of the time the ball is incidental to the main activity which appears to be a mass orgy of cuddling while one man holds the ball, ponders for a few seconds, and then throws it away. Then they all stop while the teams change players to give others a chance to come out for a hug. They get into a huddle and share secrets with each other, maybe sorting out who fancies whom in the opposition.

The poor commentator has so little action to report that he has to fill in more time than is actually played by reeling out lists of statistics in a highly charged voice: "Weeeell, the Minnesota Muskrats made an advance of 3.4 yards with that play, giving running-back Joe Blogowski a seasonal average of 2.8. Great performance from a guy who has just returned from injury after being sidelined for two weeks with a scratch on his little finger. But he is one tough cookie, 6 feet 5 inches and 250 lbs of solid bone and pure-bred, mid-west beefsteak, with an IQ of 15!" Or something like that.

By which time the players have told all their secrets and are itching to cuddle one another again. After about three seconds of intense hugging and gasping, the referee stops the game before it all becomes too intimate and lets the commentator get excited over another list of figures. What it all means is beyond me, but what else is there to say in a game that stops more often than it goes.

The term 9/11 is another example of the American predilection for enumeration. I first heard this used not long after the event when an American I met in New Zealand told me that so few of his fellow citizens would travel by air 'after nine eleven.' Why shouldn't anyone want to fly after eleven minutes past nine? Yet they would be quite happy to fly at ten minutes past nine! As I pondered this peculiar behaviour, it became clear from what followed that he was referring to September 11th rather than 9:11 a.m. The fact that it was spoken rather than written put me on the wrong track – it's a reasonable excuse! So now I know. Travel is a great educator.

It reminded me of those cryptic radio messages sent by cops in the movies which end with someone saying, 'Ten-four,' as if he knew what he was talking about. Seeing some cops standing around Boston with nothing much on their minds I decided to ask about 'Ten-four.' After all, I had been hearing this in films since the 1950s and still never knew what it meant.

The answer was vague. "It's just a sorta code for, 'I have received your message and understood it and there is nothing more for me to say.' It's a kinda shorthand way of saying things."

"Okay. But why is it 'Ten-four,' rather than 'Nine-seven'? What is the significance of these numbers?" They all looked blank. "Why not use the internationally recognised VHF radio practice of saying 'Roger. Out'?" No one could answer that either.

Mind you, I have a VHF radio operator's licence, but I can't explain why 'Roger' is used in preference to 'Henry,' or 'Nigel,' or let's not be sexist, even 'Agnes' for that matter.

The Americans are addicted to codes. I had the same problem when I heard someone on a TV chat show say, with considerable gravitas, "Y'know, Oprah, having kids is twenty-four seven." Now, you don't get a degree in mathematics for nothing, and I soon deciphered that this meant a parental commitment to child-raising of twenty-four hours per day, seven days per week. Been there, done that, and have two grown-up sons to prove it, so I know. I nodded sagely and muttered, "Ten-four." I was learning the language at last.

With a rapidly developing inferiority complex, it was with some relief that my brief stopover in the bewildering society of the USA came to an end. Bound for the South Pacific, I was travelling light. That was fine until my last day in Boston when the first snow fell. Drawing bemused looks from passers-by, I made my way to the airport in shorts and T-shirt, my bare feet turning blue in soggy sandals. Stoically, I showed no sign of pain as the snowflakes stung my feet. I was Scottish after all, brought up with bare legs and kilt, to suffer pain in silence and never weep. I looked at them with disdain, all wrapped up in their coats, furry hats, and boots, and strode manfully on.

After a long haul via Washington and Los Angeles, I arrived at Tahiti. The pilot informed us that the local time was 2:40 a.m. and the outside temperature was a cosy 26 degrees Celsius, with 87% humidity. More numbers. They are all at it. But that made my frozen feet happy. They could thaw out at last.

Chapter 3

LOCKED OUT ON TAHITI

Tahiti, island of love, a tropical paradise where visitors are welcomed and covered with flowers; an island populated by women described as among the most beautiful to be found anywhere in the world.

That was the image created by the first Europeans to visit these shores. Captain Samuel Wallis, an Englishman, arrived off Tahiti in 1767 in his ship, *Dolphin*. This place had everything: delicious fruit, fowl, and fish, a temperate climate, and beautiful, bare-legged and bare-breasted women with flowers in their hair, who lined the beach and tempted the sailors 'with every lewd action they could think of.' Two years later when Captain Cook arrived, he confirmed that Wallis had not exaggerated. The English were captivated by the women who bathed three times a day, shaved under their arms, bedecked their hair with flowers, and anointed themselves with scented coconut oil. Unsurprisingly, their aroma was judged preferable 'to the odoriferous perfume of toes and armpits so frequent in Europe.'

With my imagination fuelled by such images, I was looking forward to my first visit to this most famous of the South Sea Islands. As I crossed the tarmac apron to the arrivals hall, the sound of South Sea Island music drifted out in the warm night air, conjuring up images of delectable girls, swaying sensuously in grass skirts, smiling a warm welcome as they draped garlands of flowers over me. Instead, it turned out to be three overweight men, dressed in skirts, who played ukuleles and sang songs. Well, it was a welcome of sorts.

A fleet of luxurious buses waited outside the airport, their air-conditioning systems growling a cool welcome from the steamy humidity of the night. In front of the first bus stood a smiling woman of voluminous proportions, draping visitors with garlands of flowers. This looked a little more like the legendary Polynesian welcome I expected, albeit an inflated version, and I asked her if the bus was going into town.

"Which hotel?" asked the woman, lifting a garland of flowers from the clutch she held in anticipation of draping it around my neck. I explained I was looking for a backpacker's hostel, not a hotel. Her smile evaporated. The halo of flowers retreated from above my head and re-joined those in her hand. "We don't do backpackers. These buses are only for hotel guests," she muttered with the kind of look reserved for the sole of your shoes after having stepped on something left behind by a dog.

"Is any other transport going into town, then?" I asked as politely as I could muster.

"*You* will have to wait until dawn, and then you can take *le truck*."

A similarly voluminous American couple waddled over with a trailer piled high with luggage. They were the sort of people she was looking for. Ignoring me, she greeted them and showered them with flowers. I never wanted any of her flowers anyway. Guys don't wear flowers where I come from. I turned away.

"And you can stick your flowers up your big fat...." No, I'm far too much of a gentleman to say such a thing, but not too much of one not to think it. I retreated to the airport lounge to wait till dawn like the cheap-skate vagrant I was. Dawn was at least two hours away.

But Melanie was only two metres away. She smiled at me, and without any hint of disdain whatsoever said, "Hi! Care to join me?"

Melanie was an attractive American girl who had been sitting in front of me in the plane. A flight attendant with United Airlines, she was on vacation. I spent a couple of very pleasant hours in her company until her flight to Bora Bora was called at 5 a.m.

By now it was light, so I wandered out to the road and within seconds *le truck* appeared. It is literally that - a truck with the cargo deck fitted out with wooden benches for passengers. They are open-sided, with a canvas canopy to offer some protection from the sun and tropical rain. Travelling round the island from dawn till late at night, they will stop anywhere on request. They are cheap, the transport of the poor people - like me.

The short trip into Papeete was a pleasant experience in spite of the hard wooden seats. It was refreshing to feel the wind blowing in my face as *le truck* sped along the coast road, and the dark island faces of the other passengers bobbed around like puppets as we jolted along. It stopped periodically to load crates of watermelons, mangoes, bananas, and other produce destined for the local market. I got off in the centre of town and paid the driver his 300 francs. It was worth every cent, a taste of island life, much better indeed than sitting in an air-conditioned bus with a horde of rich American tourists.

Not that I have anything against rich American tourists. They're a friendly bunch mostly and they'll talk to anyone - and everyone - and that is the problem. Many of them seem to imagine that everyone within shouting distance will suffer some kind of deprivation if unable to hear what they are saying, regardless of how personal it may be. One guy, without any inhibitions whatsoever, very kindly walked about the airport departure lounge in LA to make sure everyone could hear what he was saying in a loud voice on his mobile phone: "Yeah, I miss you too honey. Heaps. Sure honey, I love you too. Of course I'll show you how much when I get home, baby. Yeah, you bet I will, ha ha ha.... Yeeaaah… (I could sense a climax approaching as he panted into the phone) Yeah, we'll make earthquakes, baby!" We don't talk like that in Scotland.

But now I was on my own at 5:30 a.m. in a strange town where the locals spoke French or Polynesian - and I could speak neither. The Lonely Planet Guide had four hostels listed in Papeete, but no street map. I wandered through the back streets trying to locate them; three had gone out of business, and I was left with no alternative but to book into the only one remaining. It was described as 'basic.'

With some misgivings, I paid my fee for a night's accommodation and was shown to a dormitory by a surly, half-Chinese woman with a face like a prune.

"Bed, toilet, kitchen," was all she said, flicking a finger in the direction of each. I wasn't impressed - more depressed. Concrete floors, concrete walls, all covered in the same dark, jungle-green paint. The dormitory slept seven: three double-decker bunks were crammed into an area measuring 3 metres square, while the seventh mattress was on top of a partitioned area at one end. Underneath that bed were a lavatory and a cold water shower.

The kitchen looked okay until I examined the cupboards. Most were locked. The ones that weren't had a few saucepans, plates, and cups - but no knives, forks, or spoons. You could cook food, but you had to eat it with your fingers. So that's what 'basic' meant. I put my pack on my bed and went shopping for some food.

It was easy getting to the shops. It wasn't so easy getting back. Papeete is a confusing town. The streets are laid out in a maze of irregular triangular patterns. The absence of right-angled turns is disorientating and the unwary traveller may wander around for ages, imagining that he is going somewhere, but getting nowhere. I have never been so lost in my life. The hostel was only ten minutes walk from the waterfront, yet every time I left the place I had the greatest difficulty in finding my way back.

By the time I did get back to have my lunch I found the hostel locked with no sign of any life around. What kind of place was this, locking me out at the first opportunity? A kindly passer-by noticed my predicament and informed me that mine host lived a few yards down the street, so I knocked on her door.

After a few moments her bad-tempered face appeared at the door and snarled, "What do you want?"

I politely pointed out that she had taken money from me in return for the use of the hostel, and I would like to avail myself of its facilities. She opened up with ill grace and retreated to her house, muttering something incomprehensible. I wasn't getting on too well with the ladies of Tahiti. What did Wallis and Cook have that I didn't?

Inside, I had lunch with Alex, a young civil engineer from Switzerland, who unknowingly had been imprisoned all morning while he had been reading Lord of The Rings in Spanish. Fluent in English, French, German and Spanish, he had now read the book in all four languages. He was killing time, having missed his flight to New Zealand the night before. We talked all afternoon and went out to dine together that evening on the waterfront.

The waterfront is the place to be in the evening. At 6 p.m. a host of mobile restaurants arrives, and tables are set out around them. It is fascinating to wander round looking at the different styles of cuisine available: Polynesian, French, Italian, Chinese, Thai, Japanese, Indian, and they offer very good value. It is also an ideal people-watching place, eating in the open air under the floodlights, with all the bustle of activity, and the trees along the esplanade all bedecked with lights.

Papeete's extensive natural harbour is a source of constant interest at all times of day, with vessels of all sizes - from traditional canoes to luxury cruise liners - coming and going. Along the sea front are stylish shops selling black pearls and high quality goods for the tourist market. Behind that facade are narrow streets with cracked pavements and smelly drains, small shops, a large and colourful market selling live chickens, dead fish, meat, local fruits, cheap trinkets, brightly coloured pareus (sarongs), and an abundance of heavenly scented flowers. The Polynesians like their flowers and decorate themselves liberally with them - men and women. A gardenia tucked behind the right ear is a signal: 'I am single and available'. Behind the left ear: 'I am spoken for.' I bought one and stuck it behind my right ear. Well, you never know! I had heard that age was unimportant to Polynesian women. In spite of the disenchanting encounters with the two females I had already met, I remained optimistic. There was still something about the place that I liked.

I liked it even more when a delightful teenage girl with a beautiful smile accosted me in the market. This was more like it: the flower signal works! Huh, she was only trying to sell me some wares from her grandparents' stall. I procrastinated, diverting the conversation from commerce to matters that interested me: lifestyle, language, and culture. We got on well, and I started teasing her a bit, and in return for the friendly banter I allowed myself to buy some of her scented coconut oil, supposedly to protect my skin from the sun though I suspected it might help to fry me. At least I would cook with a pleasant aroma.

The Tahiti Carnival was held the following night. Alex and I dined on the waterfront again, accompanied this time by Kiera, a hardy Danish girl who had crewed her way across the Pacific from Panama on a yacht, and Robbie, a Scot from Aberdeen. The Carnival passed by on the esplanade. To the accompaniment of traditional drum music, hundreds of participants of all ages paraded in scanty costumes in a colourful and exciting display of traditional dance. Dance is fundamental to Polynesian culture, and the way they move their hips… well, it is little wonder that some of the mutineers from the Bounty weren't too upset at the prospect of having to spend the rest of their lives in these islands.

After the carnival, a stroll along the esplanade in the warm night air took us to an open-air concert where two groups of Maori singers from New Zealand bashed out a repertoire of popular songs while executing some energetic choreography. I watched the crowd of several hundred people. It was now around 11 p.m. and certain things struck me. Whole families were there, with children of all ages. There was not a single beer can in sight, and no drunken or loutish behaviour. Although fast food stalls were serving snacks, there was no litter to be seen anywhere. The only people I saw smoking were Europeans. And everyone seemed to be having a good time. An event like that in the UK would have required an army of people to clean up litter afterwards.

Alex was leaving for New Zealand in the early hours of the morning, so we sat up late, talking. Anticipating job interviews on his eventual return, he asked me for advice. Having participated in so many interviews, both as employer and applicant, I felt I had something I could share with him and fell into the role of educator again. On leaving, he told me he was glad he had missed his flight two days earlier as he had gained so much from our conversations and wanted to keep in contact by email. That gave me a wee glow inside. I felt valued, and the thirty-five year age difference had proved to be no barrier to friendship.

The name Tahiti conjures up notions of a tropical paradise, but it fails to match the image. Unlike the popular perception of Pacific islands - the ones in the brochures with the swaying palms and the beautiful white sand - Tahiti has black sand. Its beaches are pulverised volcanic rock - and you simply cannot feel luxurious lying on what looks like coal dust. As Tahiti has the international airport, it is best regarded as a gateway to the other islands, and next day I took the fast ferry to Moorea. It is only about an hour's journey from Tahiti, and is one of the most beautiful islands in the Pacific.

Chapter 4

KISSING STINGRAYS

Moorea's mountains are the jagged remnants of former turbulent volcanic activity. Dramatic, mystical, surreal, it is easy to imagine the spirits of the Polynesian gods inhabiting the inaccessible, mist-shrouded peaks that soar out of the jungle.

Moorea, French Polynesia

A bus took me to my hostel on the west side of the island. The receptionist, a beautiful Polynesian girl, spoke excellent English, but dashed my hopes of feeling more welcomed here with a disconcerting attitude suggestive of inner thoughts: 'Not more tourists! Why can't they leave me in peace to do nothing all day?' It wasn't anything personal. Everyone I spoke to had the same impression.

It was a pleasant place to stay, though. The accommodation was laid out in blocks of rooms forming three sides of a grass quadrangle. The open side fronted a glorious beach garnished with bikini-clad bodies - and some wearing only half a bikini. I took a walk along the beach to take in the scenery. The lagoon was warm, and it was a joy to lie in its soothing water after my stroll and watch the sun set, its soft golden light burnishing the bare breasts of the girls who promenaded along the beach without a trace of self-consciousness.

I wasn't feeling homesick at all.

Having hired a bicycle next morning, I set off to cycle around the island. Much of the road was shaded with fragrantly scented trees, and the breeze generated by cycling had a pleasantly cooling effect. It is an island of contrasts: luxurious hotels and tourist resorts with beautifully landscaped gardens, and nearby, what can only be described as hovels where many of the indigenous population live. Their needs are simple: a roof to provide shelter from rain and sun, a mattress on the floor to sleep on, and not much else in the way of furniture.

Food is abundant: coconuts, mangoes, paw paws (papayas), limes, bananas, and pineapples growing in profusion. The lagoon is teeming with fish. Flocks of chickens run wild in the bush with roaming pigs and an occasional goat. Survival is no hardship here. The sea is always warm and the children spend hours playing in the lagoon. On Sundays, families sit in the shade or on the beach and sing to the accompaniment of ukuleles. They appeared to be very content. Who wouldn't be in this place?

So was I, as I sat on the beach under the shade of some trees having a lunchtime snack. Out beyond the reef, surfers carved white signatures on the faces of the huge, looming waves that threatened to engulf them before erupting white on the coral with a boom like a distant explosion. A few feet away on the sand, dozens of small hermit crabs bustled about at the water's edge, foraging for scraps in the lapping wavelets that gently washed the beach, the dying remnants of the mighty rollers that rose dark blue, turned green, and crested white on the protecting reef.

These islands are nearly all blessed with a surrounding coral reef enclosing a sheltered lagoon, a haven for small fish where they are safe from large marine predators. It also provides an anchorage for the small boats and outrigger canoes from which the local fishermen cast their nets to catch the fish. Either way, the fish get eaten. Most of the lagoons are shallow and littered with corals offering shelter and food for the many vividly coloured species of fish.

I enjoyed my six-hour trip round the island, but I was appalled at the lack of care of their dogs. Herds of mongrels roamed un-neutered around the houses living on scraps. They were the most under-nourished, mangy animals I had ever seen until then, and they howl ferociously if anyone walks along the road after dark.

Back at the hostel, sitting outside in the evening writing my diary, I was disturbed by a high-pitched voice: "Hello, I'm Chris. I heard your Scottish accent earlier. Not many English speakers here so I thought you might like some company."

Chris, in his early forties I'd guess, was a bachelor living with his mum. He peered at the world through thick spectacles with a permanent look of amazement. He wore a floppy hat, baggy shorts, and sandals, with socks pulled half way up to his knees. He also wore a video camera. If anything moved, he recorded it.

We didn't have a conversation. He only did monologue. He wasn't interested in me, only my ears. I tried to speak, but each interjection was ignored as he rambled on interminably. He told me he had dined in a pleasant restaurant the night before where they served excellent traditional Polynesian food, and very cheap too. Tonight, he was thinking of trying a place where they served Chinese food. That settled it. Having excused myself to freshen up, I sneaked round to the Polynesian restaurant. I hadn't been seated long before Chris wandered in with a look of triumph and sat himself down at my table.

"I thought you might try this place, so I decided to come here so you wouldn't have to eat alone. My mum says it's much better to have company at dinner..." and so the monologue continued. At least I didn't have to make an effort - as long as my ears were there he just droned happily on. His incessant soliloquy encouraged me to have an early night.

I breakfasted with a lovely couple from Ireland, Ann and Dan, whom I had met the night before when I sneaked into the hostel kitchen for a nightcap after I had escaped from Chris.

They invited me to join them on a lagoon cruise. We were welcomed at the booking office by our smiling skipper. Yes, the boat would be leaving soon and we would be able to swim with the fishes, feed them, and have a picnic lunch on a small island. Ann asked him when the boat would return. The Polynesians have a sense of humour.

"About 1:30." Then his eyes narrowed. He looked meaningfully at a picture of a great white shark on the wall and added ominously, "Maybe." His face creased in a dazzling smile. "No, don't worry, that is only one of our sardines. Just go down to the beach and you will see the boat. It's name is... *Titanic.*"

The boat was a modern version of the traditional island canoe: long and narrow, with an outrigger on one side, it was powered by a 50 HP Yamaha outboard engine. Our skipper kept the banter up throughout the cruise and ran a happy ship. At our first stop, he cast some scraps of food into the sea: within seconds the water was boiling as a school of small fish gorged themselves in a mad frenzy.

"What kind of fish are they?" asked one of the passengers, as we prepared to enter the water with our snorkelling masks.

"Piranhas," was the nonchalant reply. Then, with a big grin he added, "but don't worry - we only have vegetarian piranhas here."

After a spell of snorkelling with sharks - not great whites, but small, black-tipped reef sharks, maybe a metre and a half long and quite amicable - we moved to another spot. Here the water was only about a metre in depth. The skipper threw some food on the water and again, within seconds, dark shadows swept through the shallow water. About twenty large stingrays were milling around us. Casting doubts aside, we jumped in beside them. They rubbed against us, as a cat would do, and even shoved their faces up out of the water for a kiss on the nose. They looked pleased to see us.

"Of course they are pleased to see you. They know you paid 2000 francs to come and see them. That's why they want to kiss you," quipped our host.

On arriving at the beach for our picnic lunch, I waded ashore carrying a bundle of pineapples. As I grabbed the bunch, a large spider darted out from the leaves and fell on to the water. It skated with lightning speed across the surface and disappeared between my legs. I looked behind me, hoping to see it heading for the shore, but there was no sign of it. The thought that it may just have climbed up the leg of my shorts occurred to me, but I remembered that there were no deadly spiders reputed to exist on these islands. I couldn't feel anything between my legs so I waded ashore with the fruit, wondering.

Suddenly, I felt a rapid tickling sensation up my back and over my left shoulder and just caught a glimpse of a black flash as it shot up my cheek and under the wide-brimmed hat I wore to protect me from the sun. Feeling slightly uneasy, I asked Dan to have a look under the brim. Ann gasped and retreated a few paces, her hands held up over her mouth in horror.

"Oh my God, there's a huge spider hiding under the brim of your hat!"

I remained calm. Dan took his baseball cap and flicked the spider onto the sand where it scuttled away into the bush.

"Oh John, how could you be so cool?" asked Ann, overcome with admiration, "I would have died."

"Och, it was only a spider," I replied nonchalantly - and sat down before my legs gave way.

Lunch was a superb fruit and coconut salad with fresh pineapples, grapefruit, limes, and melons, all prepared under the shade of the palms of a small island with a pristine beach. Our skipper demonstrated how to husk a coconut, a useful skill in these islands where the coconut can supply both food and water. *Titanic* did not sink that day, and even if it had, we would have been able to walk ashore, so shallow was the lagoon.

I spent another day kayaking on the lagoon, swimming, and in the evening attended a traditional dance show. Against the background of an ancient marae - a temple site - the local 'warriors' presented an impressive display of the ancient art of fire-dancing, accompanied by the elegant hip-swaying of the girls.

Chris had insisted on accompanying me again. He had booked a seat at a performance a few nights earlier, but claimed the transport that was to pick him up had failed to come for him. I had the distinct feeling that no matter what he tried to do, it would end in some kind of failure. At least he was quiet this time, preoccupied with recording the dancing on his video camera - until it ran out of battery power half-way through the show!

I took the ferry back to Tahiti with the intention of taking the cargo boat, *Vaenu*, from Papeete to Bora Bora, an overnight trip of about 19 hours. The woman in the shipping office could speak no English. I tried very hard with my limited French, but all I got was a deadpan look. I persisted. Eventually, her hands moved in imitation of large waves and she said, "Pas de bateau aujourd hui." My school-learned French could understand that. There would be no boat today because of rough weather. It didn't seem that rough to me, but the boat had to call in at several islands and enter lagoons through narrow, shallow entrances, so it was maybe better to be prudent as there was a big swell running.

I groaned at the thought of spending another night in Papeete at Chez Madame Sour Face, but the only other option was a hotel - and they don't come cheap on Tahiti. I plodded back in the hot afternoon sun and booked in for another night. Her demeanour hadn't improved in the time I had been away. However, I was welcomed back by Roy, a Canadian writer who had rented an upstairs single room and was working on a book. I had met him last time there and we went out to dine together on the waterfront that evening. I enjoyed his conversation. He was having more success with the local ladies than I was and had arranged to meet one of them later so I returned to the hostel alone at 8 p.m. It was already locked.

I took perverse pleasure in hammering on Madame Sour Face's door once more, greeting her with a cheery smile, and a jolly, 'Bon soir.' My pleasant greeting was received with more muttered curses, and my darker self silently suggested that she could go and indulge in an act of self-copulation. It was only next morning when talking to Roy that I learned you could have a key if you paid a deposit of 500 francs. Why didn't she tell me about that? Still, it gave me some pleasure in knowing that she had been disturbed yet again due to her own senseless lack of communication. However, the pleasure of being on this exotic island was palling. I was looking forward to getting away again.

Chapter 5

LONELY ON BORA BORA

I t was a relief to climb aboard the *Vaenu* at last even though the vessel was, to put it kindly, rather geriatric in appearance. Various dents in the hull, some holes in the toe rail where the rust had eaten its way right through, and a prominent inward bend in the passenger guardrail did not inspire confidence in the ship, or the crew. Nor did the cleanliness of the ship. After leaning against the guardrail, having tested it first with a few hefty pushes and pulls, I came away with a dark, greasy stain on my shirt. *Vaenu* was a dirty old cargo boat, and passengers were an encumbrance to be tolerated rather than cared for.

A leaflet offering details of the voyage proclaimed that passengers could eat in the ship's restaurant, whether or not they bought food from the ship's galley. With this in mind, I had decided to keep my pack light and had not brought any food with me, other than an orange and a tin of peanuts for snacking on. I would buy dinner on board. On a voyage lasting 19 hours they must provide food. I took my seat at a table, but there was neither sight nor smell of any food.

After waiting for some time, watching others eating snacks they had brought with them, I went searching for the dour, enormous woman who masqueraded as a stewardess and was told bluntly, "No food."

"But this leaflet says…"

"No food!" She glowered at me aggressively. I backed off. I am not a timid sort, but this big woman made Mike Tyson look like a pansy. Now I understood why someone had defaced the underside of the bunk above mine by writing, 'Big Fat Cow.' Where were all the fabled, eager to please, Polynesian girls described in the tourist brochures? Dinner that night consisted of half an orange and some peanuts. I kept the rest for breakfast as the ship didn't dock in Bora Bora till 11 a.m. It wasn't very filling, but I exercised mind over matter. I had been brought up on wartime rations after all.

Despite the deprivation I enjoyed my cruise. As well as cabin passengers, the ship also takes deck passengers, mainly islanders, who sleep on mats on the after deck, protected from the weather by a canopy stretched overhead. I had tried to book as a deck passenger, but was told there was no room left. This meant I had to pay three times as much for a cabin - but the hot shower was very welcome.

I shared my cabin with a French banker from Paris. A football enthusiast, he wanted to improve his English, and I was trying hard with my French, so we got on very well. He asked me what I thought of the people here. I replied diplomatically that there seemed to be something lacking in their concept of service, but perhaps it was because of my difficulty with the language. He shook his head. "I find that too. They are not very sympathetic," he claimed.

He was travelling with his sister, Marie, and her husband, and we all met on deck in the evening to watch the sun setting behind the mountains of Moorea. A mile off on the port side, the elegant, modern American sailing ship, *Wind Song*, cast a beautiful picture with her sails silhouetted against the dying light of the sun. It was all very... South Pacific.

My French friends were considerate, and helped me in my efforts to speak their language. I had forgotten so much of my school French that at one point I struggled to say, 'I think.'

Marie came to my aid: "Je pense," and then she added by way of example, "Je pense, dunc je suis."

My eyes lit up. "René Descartes. Philosopher and Mathematician. I think therefore I am, or, as he wrote it in Latin, *cogito ergo sum*." I just can't prevent my classical education from surfacing from time to time.

"Ah, il'y connait!" she replied, beaming. "Nous avons un connaisseur de philosophie."

I bowed my head in acknowledgement of the compliment she had paid to my knowledge of philosophy, but to pre-empt her delving any further and exposing its limited extent, I added, "Oui, mais seulement un peu. J'étais un professeur de mathématique, mais je suis retraité et maintenant je suis en vacance perpetuélles."

For those of you who know less French than I do, that is supposed to mean something like, 'Yes, but only a little. I was a teacher of mathematics, but I am retired and now I am on a perpetual holiday." However inappropriate the idiom may have been, they seemed to get the gist of what I was saying.

I had a very clear recollection of exactly when I had first learned about Descartes. It was in 1957 at Irvine Royal

Academy that my French teacher, Howard Matthews, introduced me to Descartes' famous words. Little did I think then that it would impress a pretty French girl on a dirty old cargo boat in the South Pacific almost fifty years later. But that's education for you.

There wasn't much to do on board the *Vaenu* - there wasn't anything to do - so we all retired early. I enjoy sleeping on ships. The steady rhythm of the engines and the gentle roll of the long Pacific swell had a soporific effect, and I was soon asleep. In the early hours I was aroused first by the absence of any roll, which indicated that we were in the sheltered water of a lagoon, and shortly after that a change in the beat of the engines signalled the approach to the harbour. It was the first of the island stops. Then came the rattle of the derrick as the cargo was unloaded. The engines picked up a few revs and we were on our way again. These were the sounds that punctuated my sleep, and indicated our passage through the night, as we stopped at three other islands.

Having eaten the remaining half orange and peanuts for breakfast, I went out on deck. There in the distance lay Bora Bora, from where two canoes of Polynesian sailors had set out on a long voyage to establish a settlement on Hawaii 1500 years ago. Another dramatic, mountainous island with a superb lagoon and glorious white beaches, it is only about 20 miles in circumference. The arrival of American forces during World War II had a significant impact on its economy, lifestyle - and its population growth - and it is now a popular holiday destination catering mainly for American and Japanese tourists.

I was welcomed at the harbour by a cheery woman in a minibus who took me to my hostel. She told me I was the first Scot she had ever met - and she seemed pleased about that. The hostel was more of a holiday village, with self-contained bungalows, chalets, and one spacious dormitory block which slept eight.

I shared the dormitory with a couple of sculptors from Easter Island. The descendants of the men who had created the enigmatic moai on Easter Island, they were masters of their craft and had been awarded a commission to create sculptures for a millionaire's island home on one of the small islands fringing the lagoon. The pictures they had of their work were impressive, both in the scale of some of the pieces and the imaginative blend of tradition with contemporary influences. I was impressed - and there's not all that much in the art world that does that to me. I had fun practising my French with them and earned the compliment, "Hey, my Eçossais friend, tu parle Francais très bien!" Très bien maybe, but I wished I could speak a bit more of it.

Bora Bora boasts an exceptional lagoon so I booked a cruise. As well as snorkelling with the sharks and rays again, this allowed me to view the entire island from the sea as the boat motored all the way round within the shelter of the reef. We hadn't gone far before an ominous looking cloud obliterated the sun, and a ferocious squall blew in from the sea. The skipper issued oilskins to us all and we sat huddled together with our backs to it. Thankfully, it passed over in a few minutes just as we beached the boat on one of the small islands, where an excellent barbecue lunch with fish and chicken and all the usual local vegetables and fruits was provided.

Bora Bora, French Polynesia

Polynesians have a long tradition of tattooing, and someone asked the skipper about the significance of these. He explained that they were once indictors of a person's status in society. A chief would have a certain pattern, his sons something else. You could tell who the boatbuilder was. A married woman could be identified from a single girl, and so on.

"But now it doesn't mean anything," he said disdainfully. "When the Methodist missionaries came to the islands they destroyed our culture. Our music and dancing was 'sinful' and our women had to cover their bodies and wear European clothes." He rolled his eyes heavenwards and shook his head scornfully. "When the white man came here he spoiled everything."

The hostel staff were friendly here. Each morning, as I sat outside eating my breakfast, the girls from the office called out, with a big smile, "Bonjour, John. Comment ça va?"

Now that intrigued me, because I was the only one they greeted by name. The others just got a 'Bonjour.' They were also chatty each time I returned from my wandering, asking what I had been doing and how I was enjoying my stay. I complimented Nir, the manager, on the friendly service of his staff. He was an Israeli who spoke fluent English.

"Ah John, you are just getting back what you give to them. The others come here, just do their thing, and that's it. But you come with a friendly smile and always talk with the staff. You try to speak their language and they appreciate that. And you are the first person from Scotland we have ever had here. To them, with your fair hair and fair skin, you are exotic…And your accent - that's something special."

That accent? Exotic? Hmm… I'd never thought of myself as exotic, but I could get used to the idea. "So maybe there's hope for me yet to impress a vahine manea (beautiful woman)?" I had picked up some important Polynesian words too.

He laughed. "I would say, if you stick around here, your chances of getting yourself a nice Polynesian girl are very good."

The general standard of accommodation of the islanders here was higher than in Moorea. Most people are employed in tourism. The island is rich in luxurious beach resorts patronised by the rich and famous: film stars, astronauts, US presidents, and playboy princes. It is a favourite for honeymooners. At times I felt like an interloper on Noah's Ark. Everywhere, couples strolled hand in hand - I was alone. What they had, I had lost, and it hurt still. I plunged into the sea and swam vigorously across the bay to drown the anger and grief which welled up inside me.

After the swim I walked along the beach to dry off in the afternoon sun. I stopped to look at a boat drawn up on the sand and was immediately hailed by a man sitting nearby with his wife. "Hey, you want to buy?"

I declined, explaining I already had a boat. They seemed interested in me, introduced themselves as George and Marie, and started asking questions. With their French with a little English, and my English with a little French, we became friends and they invited me to join them and have a beer.

They asked me to stay and have dinner with them and took me to their home to meet Granny. Marie said something in Polynesian I didn't understand and Granny's mouth opened in a toothless laugh. She nodded her head in agreement. George explained: "My wife tell her mother you *très exotique*. She like your fair hair and skin, and her mother think you very nice too…But, hey John, remember… she *my* wife!" And he roared with laughter. That was more like the Polynesian welcome I had expected. Nir's words came back to me. I was getting used to being an exotic creature.

After five days, I decided to move on, cutting my time in French Polynesia from 3 to 2 weeks. When I announced my departure to Nir he said, "John, we'll all miss you." He didn't have to say anything, but the fact that he did made it all the more appreciated. I felt quite sorry about going, but it was an expensive place for a backpacker and there weren't many around.

I flew back to Tahiti and connected with a flight to Rarotonga in the Cook Islands at 3:40 a.m. The flights between the different island groups always seem to be in the middle of the night, but it was better than spending another night being locked out at Chez Madame Sour Face. And whatever French Polynesia lacked, the Cook Islands had in abundance.

COOK ISLANDS WELCOME

I t was 5:20 a.m. and dawn was just breaking when the Air New Zealand Boeing 767 whispered over the reefs and touched down gently at Rarotonga. In the terminal building the immigration officer looked at my passport, his eyebrows raised with interest.

Avarua Harbour with the remnants of ancient volcanoes in the background.

"Scotland? You have come a long way. Welcome to the Cook Islands. How is your rugby team doing these days?" They are keen on their rugby here, but he was asking the wrong guy. I'm a soccer man. He smiled, and passed the passport back. "Have a good holiday in the Cook Islands." And it sounded, and looked, absolutely genuine.

I passed into the arrivals hall and moved towards a lady holding up a card with Tiare Village printed on it. Wearing a garland of flowers on her head, she greeted me with a smile. "John? Kia orana. I am Mata. The minibus is over there. I have one other passenger to collect." She then planted a fragrant Tiare Maori (gardenia, the national flower) behind my ear and brushed my cheek with a welcoming kiss – and hey, I was only a backpacker! How very different from my arrival in Tahiti.

Tiare Village Hostel: swimming pool

The other passenger was Kenny from Liverpool, a short-legged, stocky character, crouched under the biggest backpack I have ever seen. Viewed from behind, he was a rucksack with feet. Here was another comedy character, an incessant talker whose speciality in the art of conversation was repetition. "This is a great place, this is. A great place, a real 'ome from 'ome. Yeah, a real 'ome from 'ome. I was 'ere three years ago. Best place in the world, this is. Best place in the world. A real 'ome from 'ome, it is. I was 'ere three years ago and couldn't wait to come back. I never felt so much at 'ome anywhere. A real 'ome from 'ome it is. It's a great place this is, a great place." There was certainly no chance of missing anything he said - and he never stopped.

Travelling alone but never lonely. Many lasting friendships were made at Tiare Village hostel.

Mata made a mistake and placed me in a single room in a chalet instead of the dormitory. She suggested we should both try to catch up on sleep and could check in at 10 a.m. When we checked in, the hostel management transferred me from the chalet into the dormitory. That was where I wanted to be anyway. It was two dollars a night cheaper - and I sleep much better knowing that I am saving money at the same time. A guy called Dave-in–the-bus (he lived in an old bus in the grounds) drove us into town to show us shops, bank, pubs, where to hire motorbikes… every place that we needed to know about. How different from Tahiti! I was beginning to believe Kenny. It was a great place. A real 'ome from 'ome.

Avarua, main centre of population on Rarotonga
and capital of the Cook Islands.

Small motorbikes are the most popular form of transport on the island. If you don't already have a motorcycle licence, you have to take a driving test to get a Cook Islands Driver's Licence.

You report to the Police Station and an officer indicates the route for the test. Drive round the block, four left turns, until you have arrived back at the police station. If you manage not to get lost, (and some people do!), haven't killed anyone on the way, and arrive back alive, you pass.

I passed, feeling quite confident in my ability to make left turns, but wondering how I would fare if I had to turn right. However, my mathematical background enabled me to solve that problem. The road is circular, running right round the island, so you can just carry on until you are back where you started without the need to turn right at all. It takes about an hour, but what does that matter? Here they live by island time. Punctuality is a concept they have yet to embrace.

That evening, Dave offered to drive us to a local restaurant to see a show of traditional Cook Island dancing and music. A few more people had arrived during the day and we all went out together, a pattern that was repeated throughout my stay there. The dancing was a delight. Beautiful girls with garlands of scented flowers crowning their heads, long hair flowing down their backs, a pair of coconut shells to cover the forward superstructure, and low-slung, grass or cotton skirts clinging to their hips - *this* was the south sea islands as I had imagined them to be. Arms and hands carved pictures of poetic grace, symbolic of the traditional fable associated with each dance, while hips swayed to the music of drums, guitars, and ukuleles The male dancers looked pretty good too. Their energetic warrior dances had a similar effect on the female members of the audience.

Some visitors pour scorn on these cultural displays as trash for tourists, but it keeps their traditions in dance and music alive. It offers the young people a healthy activity in the evenings. It is physically demanding and they practice long hours to achieve high standards. They attend international cultural festivals, not only in the Pacific region, but also in Europe, and the USA. The dancers displayed a clear enjoyment of their art, and I found it was impossible not to be moved by it all.

Once again the sense of humour of the islands' people was in evidence as the compere introduced each dance. The finale was always an invitation for audience participation, each dancer selecting a partner from the audience.

"Let me remind our visitors, you are not allowed to refuse an invitation in the Cook Islands. Shaking your head sideways means 'yes' in the Cook Islands. Nodding your head up and down means 'yes' in the rest of the world. So no matter what you do we take it as 'yes.' We don't understand 'no' in the Cook Islands… Maybe that's why I have twelve children!"

The visitors selected to dance were invited to introduce themselves and offer their dancing partners a traditional embrace and a kiss on the cheek, but with one exception. "Okay, Mike from New Zealand, say hello to Krystina, but Mike, wait! No kissing for you. That's my daughter." When the girl ignored this and planted a kiss on the young man's cheek to which he responded warmly with a hug and a peck on her cheek the MC roared, "Hey, Mike! I told you no kissing. Get your hands off!" He then made a gesture towards the band, all big fellows: "Mike, meet the brothers!" After a pause for laughter: "You got a credit card, Mike? Okay. 20,000 dollars and she's yours."

Krystina: Flower over the right ear - 'I am available.'

The drums beat their intoxicating rhythm, the dancers wiggled and swayed, their hapless partners tried their best, and the rest of us laughed. It was all good fun.

Afterwards, I had the opportunity to congratulate some of the dance team who joined in the open dancing that followed. On hearing I was from Scotland, Krystina's eyes lit up and she told me she had danced at the Edinburgh International Festival the previous year, one of a dance team from the Cook Islands who had performed before audiences of 10,000 people on the Castle Esplanade as part of the Military Tattoo. You don't get invitations to perform in the largest festival of the arts in the world if you are just offering 'tourist trash,' and that year the Cook Islands dancers took Edinburgh by storm with their scintillating performances.

"It was an awesome experience," said Krystina. "You come from a very beautiful country." A charming girl with absolutely no pretensions, self-assured, and socially mature, I would have loved to talk more with her, but the music was loud and I left her to dance with her friends. However, we were soon to meet again.

The friendliness of the islands seemed to rub off on its visitors who were equally affable. Tiare Village is by far the most sociable hostel I have stayed in anywhere in the world. It had a family atmosphere with most of the guests mixing well, socialising around the swimming pool, and grouping together for outings, day and night. The following evening I was relaxing on the deck when Kenny called out. "Come on grandad, we're going out for a drink!" I hesitated.

"Yeah, come on John, you're coming too," urged Lorna - she was harder to resist. Beautiful, blonde, and wearing...

well, I don't really remember, except that it was not very much at all… she took my arm and hauled me (but I didn't offer too much resistance) on to the pillion of Kenny's bike, and off we went. I had mixed feelings about a night out with youngsters in their early twenties. Especially when they took me to a karaoke bar.

Now, let's face it, karaoke is positively the lowest form of 'entertainment'. There was no way in the world I would ever consider becoming involved. No way. Not me!

A couple of drinks later - combined with Lorna's seductive charm - and there I was at the mike, crooning the old Elvis Presley song, 'Love Me Tender.' I gave it my best shot and got so carried away doing the Elvis impression that I lost track of the words, but, like a real pro, and without a break in rhythm, I made up a few of my own till I could pick up the thread again. I finished to rapturous applause - well, it sounded rapturous to me.

The female announcer growled lustily into the microphone, "What a performance! Oh John, marry me!" That brought more rapturous applause from the audience who then showered me with congratulatory remarks as I made my way back to our table.

Lorna got out of her seat and gave me a lingering hug, "John, you're a star!" Her eyes glowing with admiration (or was it just the effect of the vodka?), she then asked me what I had done for a living before I retired. This is the question I dread.

"I was the head of a secondary school."

"Bloody 'ell!" she exclaimed in disbelief in her broad Lancashire accent. Stereotypes. Headmasters are not expected to behave like that.

Punanga Nui, the open-air market where local fruits, vegetables, and crafts are sold, is a great place to meet people on Saturday mornings. It is almost obligatory to be there, and that day it held an added attraction - the opening ceremony of the annual flower festival, The Tiare Pageant - with the initial appearance of the contenders for the title, Miss Tiare. Six local teenagers presented themselves as contestants for the title, and eventual crowning as Queen of the Pageant after a week of performances of singing, dancing, dress, public speaking, and interviews. The girls, all beautifully dressed in colourful pareus, paraded along a catwalk and briefly introduced themselves. Number six was Krystina, whose performance as a dancer and whose maturity, poise, and friendliness had created such an impression a few days previously. I was amazed. She was only 15 years old.

Punanga Nui Market.

She impressed me again with her self-assurance and public speaking ability and afterwards, as all the girls lined up for photographs, I had an opportunity to congratulate her once more. I had forgotten to take my camera, but Mii, her mother, invited me to join them on the beach that afternoon for a photo shoot. I did not require any persuasion and, as well as the pleasure of taking photographs of a beautiful girl in a dream setting by the lagoon, I had the chance to talk with her once more. I have met many youngsters in my career in teaching, but very few of her age impressed me as much as this girl did. It came as no surprise that a week later she was crowned Miss Tiare. Four years later, she was crowned Miss Cook Islands, and went on to win the Miss South Pacific title as well. Mii and Krystina were my first Cook Islands friends. I had no idea at the time, but they were the daughter and grand-daughter of a queen who, on a subsequent visit, would invite me to be her guest on Mitiaro, one of the small outer islands.

Attending a church service, if for no other reason than to listen to the magnificent singing, is one of the outstanding memories of a visit to the Cook Islands. Traditional hymns are sung in the Maori language with obvious and infectious pleasure, often unaccompanied by music. They are so rhythmic and resonant, with male and female voices singing different parts. The order of service is similar to that of the Church of Scotland, so I felt quite at home. A nice touch, typical of the friendliness of the islanders, was the projection of the words of many of the hymns on to a screen so the visitors could participate in the singing in Maori.

Dress for church is formal: modest, yet striking compared to the sombre shades of dress in Scotland's kirks. It is not uncommon to see men wearing white, yellow, green or bright blue, as well as dark coloured suits. The women usually wear white dresses, with hats woven from dried pandanus leaves, uniquely decorated with bright flowers. This presents an aspect of purity and humility, yet is characteristic of their celebration of the natural resources of their islands, particularly the flowers.

Flamboyant Tree.

Flowers are abundant, and their bright colours are reflected in the forms of dress as in these pareus.

Hand-made hats are worn to church, each one unique.

After the church services, the visitors are invited to the church hall for a buffet lunch. Several church members join in, so typical of the friendliness that abounds here. In a welcoming address by an elder of the church, the visitors are told of the turbulent, cannibalistic past of the islands before Christianity came - when 'having visitors for lunch' meant that they would be on the menu! This hospitality is now an expression of the islanders' desire to adhere to the Christian principle of brotherly love. The food is prepared each week by a group of 'mamas' and there is always plenty of it. It was here that I met a lady who became one of my great friends, Aunty Nancy, who insisted on taking care of me and kept filling my plate with more delicacies, a trait characteristic of the Cook Islanders.

While we chatted, Aunty Nancy's niece introduced herself. Ina was a former college of education lecturer in New Zealand. Now widowed with a grown up family, she had returned to finish her career teaching on her home island. She offered a lift back to the hostel to anyone without transport. I had my motorbike, but some of the others went with her, and by the time I arrived back she was already sitting on the deck eating fruit with the youngsters. We sat there all afternoon talking with her, after which she invited us all for a barbecue at her home a few days later.

Seventeen backpackers drove out in a convoy of motorbikes, taking something for the barbecue, but she had an enormous spread laid out for us. She had also invited her relatives and neighbours to what turned out to be an international gathering of people of all ages. For many of the younger backpackers this was an eye-opening experience. They responded magnificently, helping to clear up and wash the dishes, and they all thanked her profusely on leaving. Before I left, Ina cajoled me into staying a little longer.

"John, please sit down and have a cup of tea with me. I just want to sit and talk for a few minutes to wind down. It has been such a lovely evening. It was just like having my family with me again. All these young people remind me of my own daughters, and they were all so charming." I felt like a headmaster again, getting a favourable report on my pupils' behaviour.

On my second Sunday at church, Aunty Nancy invited me to join in the evening service as well, and again there was a feast to follow. After the dinner, a form of Bible study was conducted, and I stayed on to witness that. Being conducted in the Maori language I had no idea what was being said, but Nancy explained in broad terms what it was all about. Challenged by the minister to discuss the message of psalm 121, several men in the audience stood up and spoke with such conviction, oratorical skill, and humour that the language difficulties seemed irrelevant. Without knowing a word that was said I still found it inspiring.

Interspersed with these discourses, groups of women erupted with apparent spontaneity into rousing songs, the powerful rhythm inspiring other, usually elderly, women to take to the floor and dance, their expansive hips swaying sensuously to the music, drawing smiles of amusement from the audience and the two ministers. It was all so contrary to the stern Calvinistic attitudes portrayed so often in Scotland, where such behaviour would be unthinkable. These people obviously enjoyed their religion. I recalled a few words spoken in English during the first sermon I heard on Rarotonga, "If you're happy and you know it, then you really ought to show it." They certainly did.

There was no doubt, this place did live up to the claims I had read on a website before I left Scotland: *The people of the Cook Islands are well-known for friendliness, openness, and a gentle, easy-going spirit and will happily introduce themselves with their local greeting, "kia orana" (may you live on).*

One writer described Rarotonga as *a dream island of white sands, clear Pacific waters, a reef teeming with fish, lush green forests, seemingly limitless flowers, and fresh fruits, but its greatest asset is its people - who can only be experienced to be believed.*

I couldn't agree more.

Chapter 7

AROUND RAROTONGA

Is there any nation on earth more endowed with eccentrics than the English? I can understand grown men wanting to play with model railways, but to own your own railway with a full-sized steam locomotive on a small tropical island in the South Pacific almost beggars belief. Yet this is exactly what I discovered on Rarotonga: a puffing, hissing, smoke-belching, steam locomotive resplendent in green livery, standing at a station on a railway line in the owner's back yard!

English-born lawyer Tim Arnold met a Cook Island girl in New Zealand, married her and settled on the family land on Rarotonga where he now practices his profession. That's the weekday job. His weekends for over ten years had been spent renovating a magnificent 50 year-old steam locomotive in his backyard and building the railway line and station so he could play with his toy when it was ready to run. Bought in Poland, it had been shipped to Auckland and then on to an inter-island freighter to Avarua, the only harbour on Rarotonga. Craned off the ship, it had travelled the last few miles to his back yard by road transport. Now it stood hissing impatiently on the track. It didn't have far to travel with only 150 metres of track between the buffers!

However, that was enough to enable me to realise a boyhood ambition to become a train driver. Growing up in the age of steam, I had gazed in wonder at those mechanical monsters belching out clouds of sulphurous smoke, their wheels, connecting rods and pistons all smelling of steam and hot oil. Every small boy's desire was to be a train driver and here I was standing on the footplate for the first time in my life.

I asked Tim if he would let me drive, and to my delight he agreed. His 12 year-old son acted as fireman and heaped more wood into the firebox to raise steam while Tim explained each of the controls to me. I released the brake, eased the regulator down a little, the pistons hissed and the connecting rods thrust those massive steel wheels around - I was moving. It was exhilarating, belching out clouds of smoke and steam, thundering down all 150 metres of track at a maximum speed of maybe close to 10 miles per hour. I brought her grinding to a stop, then reversed back along the line and into the station without mishap. Although the round trip was only 300 metres and we never got beyond a geriatric jogging speed, a dream had been realised - and that's what counts!

It seemed incongruous that I had left Britain, where the first ever steam locomotive was built, and had travelled halfway round the world to a small tropical island, without any railway system, to realise my ambition, but the absurdity of it all tickled me. Who but an Englishman would be mad enough to dream up such an idea?

My younger son, for several years a professional diver, had tried to get me to take up diving, and my elder son had also taken a recreational diver's course. I had always been too busy with work and sailing to allow myself to become involved, but my appetite had been whetted by snorkelling and now seemed the perfect time to do something about it at last. The cost was reasonable, the water warm, so where better to do it? The final push came from Matt Malinski, an American who'd just completed the Open Water Diver's Course and whose feedback fired me with enthusiasm. To be honest, it irked me that the boys could do something their old man had not tried. If successful, I could go on to dive The Great Barrier Reef - that would give me something to brag about when I got back home!

Muri Beach. Learning to dive.

There were only three of us on the course. The other two were a likeable American couple from Phoenix, Arizona, an odd sort of place to be a diver, I thought, away out there surrounded by desert. The woman was deafening. She didn't talk, she broadcast - to the world - and ended every sentence with a great belly laugh.

"Why do you guys want to learn to dive?" asked our instructor.

"I just looove the ocean. HA HA HA HA!" She bellowed.

Her husband, by contrast, was so quiet and must have graduated with honours from the American School of Slow Talking. In a hesitant, nasal, western drawl, his words were laboriously prised out, " Waaal I…ah…. sorta …enjoy… like… ah…swimming…in the ah…pool….in our…ah…back ya-ard."

"Yeah, we-got-like-a-pool-in-our-backyard-in-Phoenix-Arizona. HA HA HA HA." The woman roared again. The words rattled out like a machine gun and laughter was the period at the end of every sentence. Mind you, it was a good thing she always spoke for husband or we'd never have got through the course on time.

In our underwater practical tests we had to descend to 12 metres to perform some exercises; disconnecting the air supply, signalling for the use of our buddy's emergency regulator, making controlled breathing ascents etc. The poor guy went down to that depth without equalising the pressure in his ears by holding his nose and blowing in the recommended manner. He suffered unbearable pain and panicked. Releasing air into his buoyancy jacket, he shot straight up again, not a clever thing to do as any air in your body expands as the water pressure decreases. By the time he reached the surface, blood was erupting from his nose. He gave up at that point and clambered into the boat before the smell of blood got to the sharks. It was a graphic reminder of the need for care and control of ascent. Discipline is essential in this activity, but the rewards are great. His wife carried on with the course and laughed her way through the all exercises, even underwater!

Outside the reef, a shelf of coral with large pinnacles and canyons lies encrusted on top of the underlying volcanic rock. The shelf gradually increases to a depth of around 30 metres at the edge of the wall where the shadowy sides of the ancient volcano fall away to the ocean floor, some 4,000 metres (13,000 feet) below, in the inky darkness. Looking over the edge was like looking into space: gloomy, mysterious, infinite. I had enjoyed an acquaintance with the sea for so long from the surface while sailing, kayaking, swimming; but diving was something altogether more intimate. Exploring this submarine wonderland was so unlike anything that could ever be imagined. I was enthralled.

The Cultural Village, a group of traditional huts furnished with displays and artefacts, offered short lectures and demonstrations to inform the tourist. It was a good place to learn more about the islands. Greeted by a smiling girl at the reception desk, I was informed that I had to book ahead as only guided tours were allowed, and, with a feast of traditional food included, they had to know exact numbers for catering. We spent a few minutes in pleasant conversation as she probed to find out more about me, all done with a charming innocence, without any sense of intrusion. When I left she expressed the hope that I would return. The following week I did.

On my arrival at the reception desk again she looked up, her lips parted in a huge smile and she said, "Oh, it is John from Scotland. I'm so pleased you have come back." Well, so was I. It gives me a wee glow to meet people who seem pleased to see me. You don't get much of that as a headmaster.

She guided me to a hut filled with historical artefacts to await the first lecture. There we learned about the migratory patterns of the ancient Polynesians, the conflicting theories about how people first came to these islands, and the story of the development of their society to the present day. In other huts we learned about fishing methods, food and cooking, herbal medicines, jewellery, tattooes, and all the uses made of the coconut tree which meets almost every need of the islander. It provides food, drink, and construction materials. The leaves are used for weaving mats and hats, and making clothing - the so-called grass skirts are actually made of its shredded bark. Pau, the traditional wooden drums, are hollowed out from the trunk (we were taught how to play them). A very informative morning, laced with humour, was rounded off with an excellent lunch of roast chicken and fish, accompanied by local vegetables, pineapple, melon and limes, all served on a 'plate' of woven leaves.

The entertainment followed lunch: traditional music, singing, dancing, with the obligatory participation of the visitors at the end. The girl at reception, now performing as one of dancers, took my hand in hers and led me on to the floor. When the drums beat their intoxicating rhythm, I gave it all I had, legs going like bellows and arms stretched out as I had seen the warriors do. She beamed and waggled her hips, then moved in close between my outstretched arms, turning slowly as she danced, her body tantalisingly close to mine. Her dark eyes, smouldering with passion, held me entranced as they looked into mine through lowered eyelids. This was getting a bit too hot - and it wasn't just the exercise. I had to call on a lifetime of stern Calvinistic discipline to keep my primitive urges under control. At last the music stopped and I was relieved of the burden of self-denial. She turned to face me again, smiled, and clasped me in a lingering embrace, kissing me gently on the cheek.

"That was great," she murmured in my ear.

Traditional dancing.

Warrior dance.

"Aye, the earth moved for me too," I murmured in hers.

She withdrew and smiled at me once more, then left the floor with the others and it was all over.

I drove back to the hostel and plunged into the pool to cool down.

Chapter 8

THE ART OF DIPLOMACY

"C'mon John, we're all going out tonight," cried one of the girls. "No way!" I had just settled down with my book. Night clubbing is not my sort of thing, but my protests fell on deaf ears.

"Oh, c'mon, you know you'll love it."

Two of the girls mounted a pincer attack, grabbed me by the arms and hauled me out of my chair. The laying on of hands worked miraculously, transforming me from pensioner to playboy. And so, I went along with them. As usual.

I like dancing. When I grew up in the west of Scotland if you didn't dance you were destined to remain single: the dance hall was where everyone met their future partners. That night, inspired by the primitive beat of the music and the seductive sway of female hips, my creativity found expression on the dance floor and I incorporated some traditional Cook Island dance movements into my repertoire.

A big, brooding Cook Islander stared at me intently. I ignored him. He still stared. I still ignored him. Cool as a cucumber, I carried on dancing. And still he stared. My eye took a few quick snapshots. It wasn't comfortable viewing. With these shoulders he would have to turn sideways to get through a doorway, his chin grew out of his chest, and his ears seemed to rest on his shoulders. The guy had no neck; probably had his head hammered into his chest over the years in the front row of a rugby scrum. Long, heavily muscled arms dangled to somewhere just above his knees, just waiting for something to grasp and crush. I knew I'd seen this guy somewhere before… In the movies - King Kong! Like a gorilla, but with the intensity of a cat stalking its prey, his eyes focussed on my every movement. I stayed cool.

Like hell I did! Maybe he was deeply offended. Maybe he was going to defend his island's traditions from irreverent assault by this pale-skinned northerner. Maybe he was going to crush me with those enormous arms. Maybe, no maybes about it, they were as thick as my thighs. No, that's not strictly accurate - they were thicker!

The music stopped. The three girls from the hostel who had dragged me on to the floor to dance with them and got me into this predicament departed to the ladies room, as they do, all three of them together, leaving me alone to face King Kong. In the film the hero always shoved the girl out first to divert the monster gorilla's attention while he bravely hid in the bushes. There was no hiding place for me. He lumbered slowly, menacingly, towards me.

I took a deep breath. My mind slipped into top gear. This called for guile, subtlety, the application of intellect. I was a mathematician, a problem solver. Now I had a problem to solve - urgently. Being of relatively slight stature all my life (I had been reared on wartime rations, after all!) I couldn't hope to compete with him physically. I picked up my drink and took a casual sip, playing it real cool, concealing my intention to throw the rest in his face as an initial shock tactic before I delivered my first strike. Even the mightiest warrior can be incapacitated by a well-aimed kick between the legs and if the family jewels were in proportion to the rest of his physique, I could hardly miss. Then I would run like hell!

He held out his hand and smiled. "Hi, I'd like to congratulate you on your dancing. What is your name?"

"Oh," I almost trembled with relief, "I'm John." I pumped his hand enthusiastically.

"Good to meet you John. I am Terry."

"Terry? You have an English name?"

"No. We spell it T-e-r-e. My full name is Teremoana Nui O Kiva. It means 'Voyager on the great blue ocean.' My ancestors were great sailors. Where do you come from, John?"

"Scotland. And my ancestors were sailors too." We had something in common. Tradition and ancestry is important in the Cook Islands.

"Scotland? You have come a long way. You are a great traveller too. I've been watching you, John. You are a cool dancer. I was very impressed."

"Oh, thank you." I bowed my head slightly in modest acceptance of the compliment. Maybe he wasn't going to kill me after all.

"We are very friendly people here in the Cook Islands, John. We like to share what we have with our visitors."

"Och aye, we're a bit like that in Scotland. Hospitality is an important part of our culture too." Recognition of common traits must help international relations, I thought.

"That's good. We are the same kind of people. So tell me John, what is your secret?"

The glass I was raising to my lips stopped short; my mouth hung open in paralysed anticipation. I looked blank. My eyes flicked sideways towards him.

"What secret?"

"Oh come on John, we're friends now. Friends share things. I've got to know your secret, man."

I didn't want to offend him now that we were friends and gave a self-deprecating laugh. "Look, I'm maybe a wee bit thick, but I really don't know what you are talking about. Can you spell it out for me."

"John, I've been watching you. You came here with three lovely blonde girls, you've been dancing with them all night - not one, but three of them! - and they are showing no interest in anyone else but you. Now, let's be honest John, how can an old guy like you attract three beautiful young blondes? I need to know your secret, man. Let's share the good things in life!"

I roared with laughter. "Well, there really is no secret. I just came with these girls from the hostel. They look on me as a sort of father figure, I suppose. Most of the young guys here just seem to want to stand and drink, but I like dancing so they asked me to dance with them. That's all there is to it."

He shook his head, unconvinced. "No John, I think you're hiding something. You must have something special to have three gorgeous girls hovering around you all night."

At that point the girls returned. "Hi girls, let me introduce you to Tere. He'd like to meet you." After a few introductory remarks I suggested, "Why don't we all move to the dance floor and cut some groovy shapes."

See, I learn fast - I'd picked up some cool talk on my travels. As we followed the girls to the dance floor, Tere turned to me. "John, you're one cool guy!"

I heaved a sigh of relief. I was still alive. I had made another friend. And my ego had received another boost. I was cool.

A few nights later, a crowd of us from the hostel attended one of the Island Night shows. It was our farewell party for Jason, a young Canadian fire fighter who'd been with us for a week. After the show, we were all leaving the car park on our motorbikes when I noticed a couple from our group, Jim and Anna, seated on their bike, having an altercation with a large local hulk who looked rather menacing. My heart sank. Everyone had been so sociable up till now and we could do without this to spoil things. I got off my bike and walked over. After all, Jim was only 21 and maybe not experienced in the arts of diplomacy. The few words I heard were enough to convince me that the situation called for some urgent action.

My attention was distracted by a voice in the shadows. "Hi John, it's good to see you again." It was Tere, holding out his hand in friendship. I hadn't recognised him in the darkness. I grasped it warmly and we exchanged a few pleasantries.

"Do you know what this is all about?"

"My friend has had too much to drink and didn't like the way the boy was looking at him." Jim hadn't liked the way the hulk was looking at Anna, but to be fair, she was configured in a way that couldn't avoid attracting attention. They were at the staring-each-other-out stage and growling like tomcats.

"Right," I said. "Let's help them both avoid getting into trouble. Can you hold him back and I'll get the boy out of here."

"Yeah, sure." The gorilla arms encircled his friend and I turned to Jim who was still sitting on the bike ignoring Anna's plea to leave.

"Get the bike into gear and get out of here – now!" I snarled at Jim and started pushing the bike away.

Jason had also seen what was happening. He roared up on his bike and grabbed the handlebar on the other side, towing him away. "Yeah, come on Jim. Drive!" Having got him rolling, that did it and he sped away.

Tere released his friend. "Well done John, you're a good man." Then he turned to his grumbling, belligerent mate and said, "Hey, lighten up. This is my friend John, from Scotland. He's a cool guy."

I held out my hand and smiled. "Glad to meet you." Okay, I wasn't particularly, but I was still operating in diplomatic mode so a wee white lie was allowed.

The hulk glowered at me for a moment, then slowly held out his hand. Through lowered eyebrows he peered at me drunkenly and registered some surprise, "You're an old guy! What are you doing here?"

I laughed and punched him playfully on the arm. "Somebody has to keep you young guys out of trouble."

His head swivelled slowly and drunkenly to look at Tere, then back at me as I walked over to my bike before my luck ran out. He raised his hand, gave me a 'thumbs up' sign and called out, "Cool."

The others had gone on to a beach party, but I'd had enough for one night. Diplomacy is a tough business and I was only an old guy after all.

But a cool one!

Chapter 9

PAIN IN PARADISE

From an altitude of 5,000 feet, I could see Aitutaki ahead, the largest of a ring of islands encircling a pale turquoise lagoon. Taking a wide sweep round the north end of the island, I dipped the starboard wing, levelled off again, and dead ahead lay the white airstrip of crushed coral. I eased her down, down, down, gliding over the multicoloured coral reefs below, over the end of the runway. I reduced throttle and we gently touched down. A quick burst of reverse thrust on the propellers to slow her down, taxi over to the terminal, brakes on, flick the switches to shut down both engines. "Alpha-Romeo-One-Seven to Rarotonga Control. Arrival Aitutaki 1419 hrs. Out." These small planes are a great way to travel between the islands. And sitting close behind the pilot, you can easily pretend you are in control. I suppose it was the same small boy within me who'd had the ambition to drive a steam locomotive. And the great thing is, the pilot did everything just as I had. He was really quite good at it.

Aitutaki is a delight, the archetypal tropical island. Part of an atoll, its pristine beaches, the turquoise lagoon, and the small islands along the reef are the stuff of dreams.

I had travelled over on the small plane with Hilde, a tall, blonde Norwegian girl who had also been staying in Tiare Village. A welcoming party consisting of one man and a wee ten year-old boy was at the airstrip to greet us and garlands of flowers were placed over our heads. The wee boy looked longingly at Hilde's blonde hair and elegant limbs and then said something in Maori which drew a big guffaw from the man. He turned to Hilde with a grin and told her, "He wants to know if you are married." Testosterone is not in short supply in the islands. A young woman from the hostel had a minibus waiting for me and chatted all the way, telling me what to see and do during my stay.

Driving around on my hired motorcycle, I was greeted everywhere with friendly waves and offers of fruit. Mangoes were dropping off the trees and the locals insisted that I take armfuls of them. They weren't trying to sell them - they were giving them away. People sat cross-legged along the roadside taking things easy, for what else is there to do in Paradise. Energetic activity is alien in such a place. As I drove past, the sight of a light-skinned, fair-haired northerner excited them sufficiently to summon the energy to raise an arm and call out, "Kia orana." I smiled and waved back. I had come to love the warm, melodic sound of that greeting.

The beaches here are among the best to be found anywhere in the world. Wandering out of the hostel in the morning with some fruit for breakfast, I sat on white sand in the shade of the trees fringing the lagoon and sunk my teeth into a ripe mango, its juices cascading down my chin. The early morning sunlight danced with joy on the turquoise water of the lagoon. This must be as close to heaven as it gets.

One of the highlights of a visit to Aitutaki is a lagoon cruise. The usual activities, swimming, snorkelling over a giant clam garden, and feeding the fish are all on offer, but exploring the uninhabited islands of the atoll was an added bonus. Here you can sense the elemental powers that create these living, growing islands and see the development of a landscape in progress. Unlike the rocky Scottish islands, which are slowly being eroded away, these islets are in the process of being formed. The pulverised remains of coral, broken off the reef by the power of the waves, has been ground into fine sand over the years, building sandbanks on top of the reef. Coconuts are washed ashore and take root, binding the sand, and reducing the risk of it all being washed off or blown away in storms. Other seeds fall and take root and the vegetation thickens, trapping more sand, and adding humus. And an island is born. This was a family of living, growing islands.

Having landed on an extensive sand bank, I strolled over to investigate such a young plantation at the far end. On my way back to the boat, I wandered along the water's edge, head down, looking for shells and odd forms of life. I got more than I bargained for when I was startled by the sudden emergence of a beautiful young woman from the sea. Slim, elegant, with long, dark hair glistening wet in the sun, her pareu, now clinging to her body, accentuated her exquisite form. Sunlight sparkled on the droplets of water that clung to her bare shoulders. It was like a dream. A mermaid. Standing knee deep in the water, she engaged in conversation with our skipper for a few minutes. When our boat headed off, she stood there waving to us, a solitary figure silhouetted against the white sand, then slowly she entered the water again until all that remained in view was the dark pinpoint of her head, like a seal. I was mesmerised.

I turned to the skipper. "Where did she come from?"

He pointed to an island half a mile away. "Over there. She is camping on that island. That's where the people of Aitutaki go for holidays. They just take a boat across the lagoon and live the simple life: swimming, fishing, eating, sleeping. They make a fire for cooking and build a kikau hut to sleep in. That's all they need. When you live in paradise, why go anywhere else?"

We stopped for lunch on One Foot Island, another uninhabited island with superb beaches. Legend has it that once upon a time some warriors were in pursuit of a man and his son who had landed on the island. The man ordered his son to walk in front and he placed his footprints on top of his son's so that only one set of prints was showing in the sand. The boy was ordered to hide among the leaves of a palm tree while the father awaited his fate below. The warriors arrived and killed the father, but having seen the footprints of only one person on the island they departed, leaving the son to survive. And so it came to be called One Foot Island. Well… it's a good yarn for the tourists.

Although uninhabited, the island has its own post office in a corner of the open-sided dining shelter, where you can buy One Foot Island postcards and have them, and your passport, stamped with the One Foot Island icon, a footprint.

While we dined on a barbecue of chicken, fish, vegetables, and fruit, the skipper took out a ukulele and entertained us with songs about virtually every country represented by the visitors. He was stumped when it came to Scotland, but he knew about the Scottish rugby team and its former captain.

"Hey Scottish!" he called to me, "Tell Gavin Hastings that Captain Perfect was asking for him." I brought him here once. Great player, and a nice guy too."

After lunch, I wandered barefoot around the island under a cloudless sky, strolling along the water's edge, with the sun glowing warm on my back. Languid palms slept in the still afternoon air, their listless fronds casting dappled shadows over white sand. Before me lay one of the most beautiful lagoons in the world, encircled by a scattering of small islands edged with magnificent beaches. Beyond the lagoon, the ocean caressed the reef with delicate white fingers. I floated on a tide of euphoria. How blessed I felt to be here on such a perfect day.

The island was shaped like a teardrop and I had now reached the sharp end, but as I turned round the point, my heart wrenched. Coming towards me was a couple, strolling hand in hand. I looked behind me. Two more couples meandered along the water's edge, their arms around each other's waists. My feeling of euphoria ebbed. This wasn't *quite* perfect. One important thing was missing – that special someone to share it with.

A wave of emotion welled up within me. My heart ached. Thoughts, like clouds, now cast shadows over the day and a hot mist filled my eyes. I turned away from the shoreline and sat in the shade of some trees, gazing out over the sea, and the memories of the girl I had loved came flooding back.

Travelling alone around the world was not a lonely experience. There were plenty of other loose cannons around and being single was never problematic. Just occasionally, like now, alone amongst others who dreamily wandered hand in hand, I was reminded of something precious that I'd once had: the intimate pleasure of sharing treasured moments with one special person. It was because she had died that I was here enjoying this most heavenly day; my pleasure, bought by her suffering and death. I wept.

As I grieved, I heard her words again, 'Make the most of every day'. Even in death she nagged me; she would never tolerate my sitting around doing nothing and the tide of emotion and self-pity began to ebb. Yes, thoughts *are* like clouds; they may cast shadows, but they do drift away. I had this side of the island to myself once more and I sat a little longer in the sunshine, soaking up the serene beauty of the place.

It had been a perfect day - almost.

Chapter 10

SOMEONE TO CARE - SOMEONE TO SHARE

Scottish visitors are rare on Aitutaki. However, I was informed by the woman who ran the hostel that Aitutaki had a resident Scot, a woman who had married a local lad. My host insisted that I must visit her and bring her news of Scotland. I followed the directions given and found myself at the most northerly house on the island. A big, handsome Maori came to the door and grinned a warm welcome, "Kia orana."

As soon I replied he knew from my accent where I came from and brought me in to meet his wife. She greeted me in the traditional Scottish manner: "Och, come in. You'll have a wee cup of tea." She was from Kirkintilloch, near Glasgow. I was curious to know how a girl from Kirkintilloch came to be living in this remote paradise in the Pacific. She had met her husband while travelling in New Zealand. Some years later they returned to the island and set up a safari tours business.

"Do you miss Scotland?" I asked. She laughed.

"You've seen this place. Would you miss Scotland? Family and friends, yes. I would love to see more of them, but it is so far away for them to visit. But the weather - the wind and rain and cold - no thanks. I'll stay here."

She had a point. When I left, they insisted I return to see them on my next trip. It was just taken for granted that there would be a next trip and a return visit was therefore obligatory. I could feel these islands working their magic on me, weaving a web from which I would find it difficult to escape. I wasn't sure I wanted to escape; a sense of belonging had already been established.

Dating from 1823, the church on Aitutaki is the oldest building in the Cook Islands, and there I found a similar passion for singing and a welcome to rival that of Avarua Church in Rarotonga. After the service, the minister came down from the pulpit to greet all the visitors personally and insisted we stay for lunch. It was a hot day and they served up gallons of ice cream for desert. They love ice cream and don't mind how it is served. I delighted in the sight of all the dignified ladies, elegantly dressed in their Sunday-best clothes, with plastic cups filled to overflowing with ice cream - and scooping it out with their fingers. Dignity here demands re-definition.

The young people began to rehearse some dances, and when I asked what was going on I was told they were practising for a youth rally to be held that evening at Vaipae, a village on the other side of the island. Again, I was invited to join them. Everything closes on Sundays so without other distractions, I drove over in the evening. People from the various churches sat in groups on benches forming an arena, but immediately I sat down on the grass, a bonnie girl in her mid-teens left her group and sat down on the grass beside me.

"Hello, it's good to see you again. I'm glad you could join us," she said cheerily, having recognised me from the morning service. She was 15 years old. How many back home would have done that, I wondered. We chatted for a short time, then she re-joined her group and the show began: singing, dancing, and dramatic activities laced with humour. In the finale, the amassed choirs sang together, including a song with the words, "Someone to care, someone to share." I felt a lump in my throat. It encapsulated everything that my experience of these lovely islands had been about and highlighted what was absent from my life. When the show finished, I stood up to go, but my arms were seized. It was Captain Perfect, the skipper from the lagoon cruise.

"Hey, Scottish, you can't leave yet. You must eat first. Hospitality is compulsory here." I was frog-marched into the village hall and the words of the song came back to me with even more meaning: someone to care, someone to share.

Two long tables were laden with food: roast chicken, tuna, taro root, taro leaves, breadfruit, vegetables, bread, fresh fruits. Having often watched, with hungry frustration, the antics of British people at buffet dinners, slowly working their way along the tables, trying to select morsels of food using spoons and forks with what they perceived was dignity and gentility, taking ages to get from one end to the other, this was a refreshing change. The crowd swooped on the tables like vultures and grabbed what they fancied: no waiting politely in long queues, no pretentious manners - no knives or forks either. You simply scooped up what you wanted with bare hands. Fingers dipped into stews and dishes of vegetables - no concern about hygiene here! And you ate with your bare hands. All the genteel manners my mother had insisted upon were discarded. The Aitutaki style suited me fine.

I took my plate of food outside and sat on the steps to eat it. Several girls in their mid-teens came over and joined me, quite uninhibited in their eagerness to satisfy their curiosity. After the usual, "Where are you from?" and "What is your name?" it got more personal.

"Are you married?" I shook my head and explained my widower status.

"How old are you?"

"Oh, far too old for you."

"Age doesn't matter." She countered, with a coquettish look to the accompaniment of giggles from her friends. I liked her quick banter, and fired back.

"How old do you think I am?"

"Mmmm, maybe forty-five?"

"Oh, you sweet-talking flatterer," I mocked, but she had scored heavily on the compliments so I conceded my age. That convinced her that I was well past my use-by date and she started to shop around.

"Do you have any sons?"

"Yes, but they are both married." She was persistent.

"Do you have any grandsons?"

"Aye. I have one who is 16 years old." Her eyes flashed.

"Is he as good looking as you?" I liked this girl even more.

"Oh, *much* better looking." My modesty is overpowering at times.

"Can I have his address please?"

The conversation turned to other matters and on discovering I had been a teacher they insisted that I visit their school next day. It would be no problem they assured me. Visitors were always welcome.

And they were right. Next morning I presented myself at the principal's office and told him some of his students had invited me to visit the school. "Yes, you are very welcome to look around. Just go and introduce yourself to the teachers. I have a meeting to attend now." It was that casual. The teachers were equally casual. It was nearing the end of term and apart from a few senior students swotting for exams, the others had freedom to go out and play football, socialise, or sit talking in classrooms while the teachers got on with paperwork. I was therefore a useful diversion.

Once again the thing that struck me was the open friendliness displayed everywhere I went. The pupils were a delight, well mannered, but relatively uninhibited. They were intensely curious about me, and Scotland, a place few could identify on a map. They had a vague notion that it was somewhere in the northern hemisphere, but that was about it. Yet they all knew about the Loch Ness Monster, kilts, and bagpipes.

It doesn't take long to establish a reputation on these islands. One of the girls approached me and said, "Hey, I know you." I laughed.

"Och no, you're mistaken, I come from Scotland."

"Ah, but I still know you," she insisted, with all the confidence of a born-again Christian with four aces up her sleeve. "You were dancing with Bibiana Paulo at the Blue Nun on Saturday night."

"Who on earth is Bibiana Paulo?"

"She's the dancer who picked you out of the audience to dance with her at the end of the show. She went all the way to the back of the room to get you. You danced with her, and she put her ei (a circular head-dress of flowers) on your head at the end of the dance because you were the best dancer among the visitors."

The evidence was overwhelming. Correct in every detail.

"Well, you can't do anything on this island without being found out," I muttered.

"Did you enjoy yourself?" she asked.

"Who wouldn't, dancing with Bibiana?"

"We noticed!" she retorted, with a laugh. "She's one of the best dancers on the island. That was quite a compliment she paid you. You danced really well." I acknowledged the compliment with my usual humility and changed the subject before I revealed any more fantasies. I was enjoying myself with these kids.

Speaking with the youngsters, I observed a contentment with their environment and culture. Only a few were concerned about leaving the island to find work. Most were quite happy at the prospect of living locally, marrying, and having families. They all seemed to love children and most had experience of looking after babies within their families, or caring for the children of friends and neighbours. You could see this in the churches, the shops, on the beaches, and at the youth rally the night before. The evidence that family is important was everywhere. It reminded me of my early life, when older girls often acted as an assistant mother, helping with the younger members of the larger families that were common over half a century ago.

At lunchtime, a few boys were kicking a football around and I joined in. The speed and agility of youth may have deserted me, but the ball skills remain and this impressed the lads.

"Will you stay and be our coach?" they asked. I was touched when they expressed dismay on hearing that I was moving on next day. "But we want you to stay," they protested. "And you'll miss our cultural week when we have competitions for singing and dancing and music. You'll enjoy all that."

I instantly regretted my decision to stay only a few days on this idyllic island, but unlike the islanders, I still had not relinquished obedience to the great ruler, Time, and next day I took my scheduled flight to Atiu.

Chapter 11

UNDERGROUND ON ATIU

Atiu is an island of raised coral, thrust out of the sea by cataclysmic forces a few million years ago. It feels rather strange to wander through forests where lush vegetation grows over what were once undersea coral reefs. Many years ago, to reduce the risk of death or damage from cyclones, the missionaries encouraged the population to move from the narrow coastal fringes up to the plateau in the centre of the island, and this is where everyone lives today in a series of connected villages.

Dinner each evening was pre-booked at the only restaurant on the island as part of the accommodation package, but I had to find some food for breakfast and lunch. In the village store I was met with the friendly, smiling faces of women happy to serve and genuinely interested in me, and where I'd come from. It wasn't the pre-packaged, mechanically smiled, "Have a nice day," of the Americanised shop girl. These people actually talked with you, smiled at you with warm brown eyes, laughed with you, told you about places to see, things to do. They hoped you would stay as long as possible and share in their way of life.

One enormous lady, with dark brown eyes the size of golf balls and bosoms that made watermelons look like peas, stopped stacking shelves to satisfy her curiosity. She wasn't being nosey: she was interested. In no time at all we were laughing and joking with each other and then she asked, "But why do you come all the way from Scotland to Atiu? How did you know we were here? It is so small it isn't even on the map.

"I had heard of the Cook Islands so I came to Rarotonga first and then I heard of Atiu, so here I am. Why did I come here? I am looking for a …", I paused, my eyes roaming up and down her massive shape and gave a seductive flicker of my eyebrows, "vahine manea (beautiful woman)… to take home with me."

Her eyes lit up, she stretched her arms out wide, "Take me!"

"Oh yes! My prayers have been answered," and I clutched her enormous body in a warm embrace. My arms barely reached round her shoulders. It was like squeezing a beach ball. No bones, just sackfuls of soft, cuddly flesh.

Then her face fell. "Oh, I just remembered - I have a husband!" I feigned misery.

"And I thought I had found the girl of my dreams," I mourned.

She roared with laughter. "Oh, you're very welcome here, Scottish man."

There are several interesting limestone caves on the island, where the kopeka, a rare species of swift, inhabits its dark subterranean world. From mud nests stuck high up on the cave walls, the tiny fledglings begin their first flight into the total darkness of the cave and, using sonar navigation by emitting high pitched sounds, they find their way out to the bright sunlight. How they adapt to the light after living all their infant lives in total darkness is another of nature's wonders.

Trekking through the dripping, humid landscape was challenging. Boots are recommended as the rocks are so sharp and I had only sandals, but being fleet of foot I had no trouble negotiating the razor-edged rocky paths. It was well worth the effort.

Our guide took us deep into a cave and ordered us to put out our headlights. Standing beside me was Jane, a lively Scottish girl who'd arrived on the same flight from Aitutaki. The darkness was total, quite unlike anything I had ever experienced, and it was destabilising. With nothing to serve as a reference point, I began to lose my sense of balance, or so I thought. I reached out to catch something to stop me from falling and touched soft, female flesh. It was an arm.

"Oh, sorry. (I wasn't really, but it seemed the right thing to say). Who's that?"

"It's me. Jane."

"Oh. Okay Jane. Me Tarzan." Laughter broke out and the lights went on to see what we were up to. Damn!

On our trek back through the bush we stopped at a tumunu. This is an illicit drinking den deep in the jungle, comprising a small hut for brewing the local bush beer and a covered area for sitting and supping. The word tumunu originally described the traditional, hollowed-out coconut stump used for brewing the beer. Alcohol was unknown on the islands until the British whalers arrived around 200 years ago. Kava, a mild relaxant, was then the traditional communal drink. Atiu had an abundant supply of oranges so the whalers brewed a sort of orange flavoured bush beer, and once the locals had acquired a taste for alcohol, well... like every other primitive society to which it was offered, they embraced it. Nowadays the beverage is brewed in plastic barrels using imported hops and orange flavouring. It is drunk only in small quantities. It is *very* potent.

Every evening a group of local men gather there to discuss the matters of the day, to sup some of their illegal jungle juice, to sing, and ease away the tensions of life - stress management, Cook Islands style. It reminded me of the bothans on the outer islands of Scotland, remote shelters on the moors where men furtively assemble to sip and socialise, fugitives enjoying a few hours respite from the perceived cruelties of a culture dominated by Calvinistic Presbyterianism.

There are several tumunu on the island, but having gained popularity with the tourists, the police turn a blind eye to their presence. Or maybe it is divine intervention. Drinking never starts without a prayer, and it struck me that there was a delightful absurdity in this. There was none of this 'give unto Caesar that which is Ceasar's' stuff here. It was only man's law, made on far away Rarotonga they were breaching, not God's law. Maybe the prayers worked. Nobody misbehaved, the police stayed away, and everybody had a pleasant time. It was all so civilised.

It was a serious, ritualistic business, at least at the start. Seated on palm logs in a circle, we were asked by the chairman for the day to introduce ourselves. When I mentioned Scotland, our chairman's eyes immediately lit up. "John, my great-grandfather came from Scotland. My name is Rory," he announced with pride. You could hardly find a more Scottish name than that, and when Jane also mentioned Scotland, he insisted on having a photograph taken with us, with me sitting on one knee and Jane on the other. It was no problem for him. He was a big guy.

Introductions over, we were then given the lore about the drink and its place in local culture - and warned about its potency. "Don't sit down for too long or you'll discover you have rubber legs. Get up and walk around after every two or three drinks and you should be OK."

It is a ceremonial affair. A small conical cup is filled from a barrel and passed to each person who swallows and passes the empty cup back to be re-filled. The process is repeated with the next person and it goes on round the circle. After a few rounds the seriousness evaporated, the guitars and ukuleles came out and the singing started. Now we were having real fun, and by the time our transport returned to take us back to the hostel we were in such high spirits we couldn't care less about dinner. However, courtesy dictated that we had to say our farewells to the boys, though with much reluctance. It had been a memorable cultural experience. Even better, there was not a trace of hangover the next morning.

On the flight back to Rarotonga, I discovered I had forgotten to hand in the key for the hostel on Aitutaki. I felt bad about that. They would have to phone the hardware store in Rarotonga for a replacement and then have it flown to the island. That wouldn't be fair. I had to get it back to them. I could mail it back, but that would take time. A better solution occurred to me.

These islands reminded me in many ways of the Scottish islands where they live by a different set of rules - bureaucracy is tolerated only when it has to be. There are often better ways of getting things done.

On arrival at the airport, I went to the Air Rarotonga desk and asked the girl, "Could you give this key to the pilot of the next flight to Aitutaki, and ask him to pass it on to the bus driver to drop it off at Papa Tom's Beach Hostel on his way round the island?"

"Certainly sir, no problem." Now that's what I call service. I was feeling very much at home here. Can you imagine going to the British Airways desk at Heathrow Airport in London when you've discovered the hotel key from New York is still in your pocket, and asking the girl to pass it on to the pilot of the next Boeing 747 heading that way, to give to the airport shuttle bus driver to drop the key off at the hotel? I might just try that next time I'm at Heathrow. It might provide a little entertainment playing the daft highland laddie after a long-haul flight.

On my return to Tiare Village I was asked by Poko, one of the hostel staff, if I had met her brother.

"I don't know," I replied. "I met a few people, but the only guy whose name I can remember was at Sam's Tumunu. He was called Rory."

"That's my brother," she replied. The Cook Islands really is a small community.

Chapter 12

FINAL NIGHT ON RAROTONGA

Ten of us from the hostel, a mixed group, singles and couples, went out for dinner together on our final night on Rarotonga. The waitress smiled and welcomed us in the traditional Cook Islands manner: "Kia orana."

"Kia orana. Pe'ea koe?" I replied. That took her by surprise. She beamed, her eyes suddenly alight with interest.

"Meitaki ma'ata. Pe'ea koe?" she replied smiling back at me, her white, even teeth contrasting with the dark colour of skin and hair.

"Meitaki au," I murmured, my eyebrows flickering upwards in an affirmative gesture. In the Cook Islands they don't just use words for communication: a variety of facial expressions, grunts and glottal stops are also part of the essential vocabulary. I hadn't frittered my time away: learning a bit of the local language is always useful. Having exchanged greetings in Maori, she chose to offer a compliment and switched back to English.

"You speak our language very well for a papa'a (a white man). Where did you learn to speak Maori?" She was nibbling at the bait.

"I've been here for a few weeks."

"You're doing very well." Then she flashed an inviting look. "You should stay longer."

This was all developing very nicely. The waitress helped us put two tables together to accommodate the whole group and re-set the cutlery. I stood back and observed as she worked her way round the table, presenting me with the opportunity to study her aesthetic qualities from various angles.

An attractive, honey-coloured Cook Island girl, she wore a floral cotton blouse and a black skirt of mid-thigh length that accentuated their gentle curve of her hips. The fragrant, creamy-white gardenia tucked above her ear contrasted with her dark hair, swept back and bundled in the style usually worn in daytime or for work. Modest, yet alluring, the subtle underplay of the hairstyle accentuated her fine Polynesian looks, a beauty perhaps enhanced by a blending of European genes to lighten the colour of her skin. My imagination toyed with images of how inviting she would look when she untied her long hair and allowed it to cascade down her back in the style worn when dancing. Well, that helped to pass the time until we were all seated.

She took out her notebook and stood closely beside me. I inhaled the subtle fragrance of scented coconut oil, with which they anoint skin and hair, as she took my order. Then, tilting her head, her brown eyes looked into mine and she asked, "Are you single?"

Was I hearing right? She didn't beat about the bush, did she? I couldn't believe my luck. An attractive Polynesian girl propositioning *me*? I'd been told so often that age was irrelevant here, that Polynesian maidens often regard the more mature, experienced European male as an attractive proposition; exotic, kinder and more gentle, more caring and considerate, more skilled in the arts of love, with an emphasis on the quality of the experience. Yes, that's me alright. And this girl was asking if I was single.

"Yes," I gasped. "And are you single?"

"Yes." There was just a hint of puzzlement in her voice. Of course, I hadn't read the signs. She was wearing the flower over her right ear.Flower on the right ear, she's single and available; on the left ear, she's spoken for - remember? The way ahead was clear. This was too good a chance to miss. I didn't beat about the bush either.

"Well, since we're both single, how about getting together after you've finished work tonight?"

She regarded me with some bemusement for a moment. "I only wanted to know if you would be paying for one meal or two when I make up the bill." My face fell and roars of laughter exploded around the table.

When I went to the desk to pay the bill, I engaged in some banter with her again. The manager, a pleasant, middle-aged woman, came over. "Enjoy your meal, sir?"

"Yes indeed," I assured her, "and I'd like to pay tribute to the excellent quality of the service. Our waitress was not only efficient and effective, but utterly charming and made us feel very welcome."

The manager beamed at the waitress. I then explained my disappointment over the language difficulty when she had been taking the order and that brought another laugh. "I've travelled all over the Pacific looking for a vahine manea and I thought that tonight my dream had come true." I hung my head. "But she turned me down."

"Oh, I'm sorry, but I will be working till very late tonight," the girl explained. The manager and the girl looked at each other. Not a word was spoken, but I could see from the looks and the eyebrows flickering that some meaningful exchange had taken place. The manager looked back at me, raised her eyebrows, and said, "She's not working late tomorrow night."

The girl looked sideways at me, her dark eyes raised invitingly. My heart fluttered. "Does that mean you'll be free tomorrow night?"

She smiled coquettishly. "I'll be at the Cocobar at ten o'clock."

"Great!" I whooped. Then… Disaster. "Oh no! I have to be on the plane to Fiji at ten o'clock tomorrow night."

She shrugged and flicked a mischievous smile at me. "Maybe you should come back some other time."

"Oh, ka 'oki au!" (Oh, I will!)

She smiled at me and murmured, "Ka kite." (See you).

Ach, but it was only a wee bit of banter. She couldn't possibly be interested in an old guy like me. Could she?

For those of you who like a happy ending, forget it. I returned a year later, but the restaurant was under new management and I never saw the waitress again.

Chapter 13

FAREWELL TO RAROTONGA

After dinner we went to see an Island Night Show. When the show finished, our dancing began. We were in a party mood and Lorraine, an Irish-born girl from Leeds, didn't need any courage from a bottle, so we were the first couple on the floor. A young American came over during a break in the music.

"Hi. I'm Roy from New York. I'd like to congratulate you. You have quite a fan club over there. There are fifteen young ladies all wishing they had boyfriends who could dance like you."

"Och well, you just tell them to come and join us." And shortly afterwards they did, shaking ass, flashing eyes, and muttering words like 'Cool' and 'Groovy.' From then on the place was jumping and by the end of the evening I had become acquainted with many more backpackers from other hostels. On leaving, a minibus from another hostel drew up beside me in the car park and hands were thrust out to grasp mine. "You're a star, John. I can't believe you were once a headmaster!" Nor could I - life was never like this at home.

I had a few things to attend to in the morning, and after returning the hired motorbike I wandered along the street with my thoughts, killing time. I regretted that I had been so busy dancing and I hadn't said farewell to Krystina and Mii the night before. As I gazed in a shop window I heard a voice behind me, "Doing some last-minute shopping?" I turned round and there was Mii, smiling at me.

"Och, I was just thinking about you. I didn't get a chance to say goodbye last night."

She invited me to join her for lunch and when we parted she said, "Now you must keep in touch."

"I will." I assured her.

Virtually the entire hostel was leaving that night, some heading eastwards to Los Angeles and then England, others westwards to Fiji. A host of backpackers from other hostels were on the move too, and the airport was seething. I felt more than a tinge of sadness, for here in the Cook Islands I had found something special among a circle of friends to whom age and nationality were irrelevant. Barriers had been removed and my future was beginning to define itself.

The social boundaries within which I had been constrained, while serving my community as a headmaster, had evaporated in the greenhouse atmosphere of backpacker life on Rarotonga. Back home, my social life had comprised almost exclusively of events at which I performed in some capacity: as an after-dinner speaker, compering charity shows, chairing meetings. I only went out if I had a duty to fulfil. I had avoided dances after my wife died: they brought back too many heart-wrenching memories.

Here the environment was different. For a start, the music was different, so it didn't evoke memories of the past, as familiar tunes often do, and I wasn't always the single man among couples of my age group. Having been press-ganged into going out on that first night, I then yielded to the exhortations of the young backpackers. That they should want me to go out with them surprised me, and I enjoyed it - which surprised me even more. I had lived in social isolation for too long, and besides, this trip was all about new experiences, and exploring the international backpacker culture was just as valid as exploring the cultures of the societies I would visit.

I was not only a curious observer, I was a participant. In the ageist society of the UK, it would be inconceivable that young people in their early twenties would want to spend their evenings in the company of a retired headmaster, boogieing the night away with him. But here it was different. One of the basic principles of biology is that behaviour is a function of environment. I was no longer the authority figure in the community that a headmaster is often perceived to be. Here, I was just another backpacker. My age and previous professional status were irrelevant. It didn't matter to them, so why should it matter to me?

Several of the friendships have endured, despite a gap measured not in years, but in generations. Jason, the handsome Canadian fire fighter adored by all the girls, but faithful to his girlfriend at home, was a mere twenty-three years old. When he left for the airport in his taxi, we followed in a motorcycle cavalcade, and when we drove off, all blowing our horns in final salute, he was almost in tears. He'd stopped off in the

Cook islands for a week on his way back home after taking part in the World Fire Fighter Games in Auckland, and had been blown away by the friendliness he had encountered here. In spite of almost forty years difference in our ages we hit it off right away, and his parting words to me at the airport were, "As long as I live, I'll never forget you, John".

He didn't. Back home in Scotland six months later, I was aroused by a phone call from Edmonton. "Hi Johnny Boy! I'm celebrating my 24th birthday and I just had to call you to hear that Scottish accent again."

"Oh, that's very nice, happy birthday," I murmured. He detected the sleepiness in my voice.

"Hey, what time is it over there?" The guy had no concept of time zones.

"4:30 a.m."

"Oh shit! Hey, I'm really sorry for wakening you up, Johnny. I never thought….."

"Ach, don't be daft. I'm delighted to hear from you, you big, daft lump. Happy Birthday!"

"Hey, when are you coming over to Canada to see me, John?"

"Oh, I'll fit in a visit on one of my trips," I assured him. I fell asleep again with a smile on my face.

Matt from Colorado, an interminable youth in his early forties, travelled the world in celebration of redundancy. Rather than feel despondent about being forced out of work, he regarded it as a heaven-sent opportunity to take a year-long trip round the world with the intention of visiting as many countries as possible, seeing everything and doing everything. Easy-going, fun loving, and a great mimic, there were always laughs when he was around. His ever-cheerful, positive attitude was an inspiration. I love the company of positive thinkers. When the time came for him to move on to Fiji, he hugged me (to my extreme embarrassment, I might add - we don't overdose on that sort of thing in the north of Scotland) and said, "John, I sure wish I'd had you as my high school principal. Keep in touch, Buddy." I did, and six months later he spent a week as my guest in Scotland during the European part of his tour.

Once again the premise that by mixing with positive, enthusiastic people you will gain so much more from life, held true. It was his infectious enthusiasm that inspired me to take up scuba diving, opening up opportunities for exploration of the amazing world beneath the waves, developing more friendships, and eventually offering a new career. My graduation as a diver may have come late in life, but it was no less satisfying. Youth had not deserted me yet.

A chat with a couple of the girls before leaving for the airport transformed into an impromptu 'Interview Tutorial' in the hostel lounge as they waited, packed and ready to go. It developed out of a conversational remark about the nerve-wracking prospect of having to face job interviews, but once the advice started flowing the backpacks were opened again and out came the notebooks. Two more then joined in. They listened and reflected, questioned and wrote notes, and frequently stopped me with remarks like: "Just say that again, John. That sounds really good. Oh, yes, I'll use that."

They began to realise that, though short on work experience, they had developed marketable qualities. They had proved themselves adaptable by travelling independently for a year or more, living in different societies with different cultural values, and in a variety of living conditions. They had proved capable of establishing effective communication, sometimes in languages unknown to them before they started, and had demonstrated the ability to get on with people and work as a team. The organisational skills necessary to deal with the logistics of world-wide travel and the ability to cope with all sorts of unexpected difficulties could be transferred to the working environment.

They began to see themselves differently. "Hey, I never realised that I could turn my travel experience to such advantage. This has been really illuminating. Thanks John." They embraced me warmly and left with glowing smiles. Like Alex on Tahiti, they were now empowered with a new confidence. I had been a teacher again and had revelled in the experience.

I began to develop a new self-awareness. Having felt so often after my wife had died that I was drifting, a piece of flotsam, the debris of a shipwrecked partnership, I was now finding a purpose in my travelling. My experiences of life could be shared and possibly bring benefit to others. I began to feel as though I may still have some worth. It brought home to me that retirement is not a human scrap yard, but an opportunity for self-development.

Another ingredient in the recipe for change came from discussions with Mark and George (Georgina), a couple who were travelling around the world together. They moved on to do volunteer work in Sri Lanka, looking after orphaned baby elephants. Having kept in touch and been inspired by their experiences in voluntary work, I became convinced that this should be a focus in *my* future travels: staying longer in one place, making a contribution to the community. I had a lifetime's experience in education to offer. Surely I could be of some use here in the Cook Islands. I had learned that Global Volunteers, an American organisation, sent tutors to the Cook Islands to help children with learning difficulties improve their English. That interested me. I spoke with the programme coordinator with a view to becoming involved on my next visit. I had already decided to come back, so I now had a real purpose in returning to the Cook Islands, to put something into a community that had received me with such warmth.

My flight was now being called. There were hands to be shaken, goodbyes to be said, and girls to be hugged. Ed, a wee Irishman, with all the loquacious charm for which his race is renowned, had a word for everyone. I was last in line. He looked at me for a moment, then grasped my hand and said, "John, for once, words fail me!" Then he disproved it. "You've put us all to shame. You'll never grow old."

As the Air New Zealand Boeing 767 soared into the night sky, I watched the lights of Rarotonga fall away beneath us, quickly becoming lost in the wraiths of cloud. With a heavy heart, I curled up under my blanket as the plane turned westwards towards Fiji. Under closed eyelids, a tide of images of the Cook Islands flooded my mind. Beautiful island beaches, glowing white under gently swaying palm fronds bordering serene, turquoise lagoons; and behind them mysterious, mist-capped peaks rising from the jungle. Playbacks of dancing, swimming, diving, bush-trekking, socialising round the pool. Laughter, with so many of the people I had met, people I could now call friends.

The unforgettably passionate singing in the churches and the generous hospitality offered afterwards. Bibiana crowning me with her ei on Aitutaki; the kids at school, chatting so freely and pleading, "We want you to stay." Rory and the boys at the tumunu on Atiu, singing and sharing their bush beer with us. Krystina, Miss Tiare, charming, and unaffected by her success, dancing gracefully in her traditional costume and Mii, her mother insisting, "You must keep in touch."

And again I heard the voices of the young people on Aitutaki singing their song: "Someone to care, someone to share." That was what I had found here among the backpackers and the people of the Cook Islands. And now I was leaving, my heart ached, and a hot mist filled my eyes.

I had been enchanted by these islands. I had to return.

Cook Islands sunset.

Chapter 14

FITTING IN ON FIJI

Fiji International Airport is at Nadi on the west side of the main island, Viti Levu. After spending the first night there it took a six-hour bus ride to reach Suva, the capital, a modern city with a population of about 150,000. The buses were just a step up the transport ladder from le truck in French Polynesia; old, battered vehicles with no glass in the window frames (it's what they call air-conditioning here) and they have tarpaulins to roll down if it rains. The buses run more or less continuously round the island, all seemed to be packed to capacity - and they are cheap.

My hosts in Suva were Ray, an Australian in his early fifties, Head of the Department of Aeronautical Engineering at the Fiji Institute of Technology, and his partner Wainese, an attractive Fijian girl. I had been introduced to them by email through a common friend, an Australian girl I had taught over thirty years previously and with whom I had become re-united through the internet. She had written to them asking if they would offer me some hospitality and help me get around.

Viti Levu, the main island, is a large mountainous mass with over three hundred small islands scattered around it. Vanua Levu, another large mountainous island lies to the north. On Viti Levu, sugar production is the mainstay of the island's agriculture.

Outside the main centres of population - Suva, Nadi, and Lautoka - the smaller towns had more of a third world appearance. Many of the buildings and streets were dirty, littered, and lacked maintenance. Drainage was poor and smelly. At the comfort stops (a real misnomer, for the toilets were far from comfortable, defying description in most cases!) fast food was available at shops and kiosks, but the grubby appearance of the premises dispelled any pangs of hunger. The shops all seemed to be run by Indians or Chinese.

The rural dwellers were indigenous Fijians, living in villages of simple bungalows made of timber or corrugated iron. Some still occupied thatched vernacular huts constructed of woven palm leaves tied to a timber frame. They had a certain ethnic charm, but little in the way of amenities. Suva was like any western city: bustling with traffic, a busy harbour, fine shops, tall office blocks, and elegant houses in the leafy suburbs.

The indigenous Fijians were friendly, smiling at me in the street and addressing me with their standard greeting, "Bula!" They were always curious to know where I had come from, if I was married, and how old I was. Fiji, at the confluence of the ancient Polynesian, Micronesian and Melanesian migratory patterns, has a real mixture of races, with all sorts of hybrids. On top of that, more recent migrations brought a significant influx of Indians and Chinese, as well as a fair proportion of Europeans.

In common with their other Pacific neighbours, the Fijians love their flowers. I had been invited to attend Wainese's graduation ceremony at the Fiji Institute of Technology. For eight hours the previous day her mother had sat on the floor intricately weaving and binding row after row of flowers into a circular garland; called a sulusulu, it was to be worn over the shoulders. A beautiful synthesis of colours, texture, and fragrance, it celebrated not only the long tradition of appreciation of an abundantly floral environment and the exuberant gaiety of these people, but also a mother's pride in her daughter's achievements. It was a work of art. Every graduate wore one, each unique, on top of their academic gowns in a colourful ceremony blending the ancient culture of the islands with the European tradition of celebrating academic achievement.

While that was a memorable occasion, it was overcome by our visit to Wainese's grandmother afterwards to let her see her grand-daughter in her graduation robes. Here, we entered what was very much a third world environment; a cluster of corrugated iron shacks only a few minutes drive, yet a whole world away, from the modern city centre of Suva.

Granny sat cross-legged on the floor of the hut, always smiling, as did all other members of the extended family who had gathered there. Children appeared, gazed in wonder, and disappeared again. It was an open house. No formality, no barriers, everyone welcomed. Ray and I shared the sofa, which with one other well-worn chair, were the only items of furniture. Everyone else sat on the floor. Bare, unclad corrugated iron sheets nailed to rough wooden supports formed the walls and roof. Windows were simply open gaps with wooden flaps to offer protection from inclement weather. A mat of woven pandanus leaves covered the floor. There was no running water, and no electricity.

They displayed none of the affected attitudes encountered in the western world where an impromptu visitor is so often greeted with, "Oh, you'll have to excuse the house." The house didn't matter. Hospitality did.

I was welcomed with genuine warmth and made to feel at home. Everyone was colourfully dressed, and despite the absence of plumbing, everything they wore was spotlessly clean. They were smiling, laughing, and at ease with their visitors. When I took photographs of Wainese and her family with my digital camera they were thrilled to see the images on its small screen. Any reserve initially displayed by the children evaporated rapidly. They hovered around me like flies, eager to see each picture as it formed on the screen, then squealed with delight at the image.

Wainese's cousin Dika, an attractive girl with two bonnie young children, sat on the floor and chatted with me. Bright, intelligent and charming, her brown eyes glowed as she looked up at me. The smile never left her face and she laughed so readily as we shared some happy banter. It was impossible not to be attracted to her.

What future might this girl have had given different circumstances, I wondered? She seemed destined to remain in these humble surroundings, would no doubt bear more children, live in poverty for the rest of her life. But poverty presents itself in many guises, of which lack of money and material comforts is but one; there is plenty of emotional poverty in our affluent western society. In spite of the lack of what we would regard as essential amenities, this girl looked clean, healthy and happy. She had two beautiful children and the support of her extended family around her. Perhaps there was something to be envied in her life.

When the time came to leave I kneeled down and kissed Granny on the cheek, much to her delight and that of her family, shook hands with the grinning uncles and cousins, and kissed Dika softly on the cheek and wished her well. She smiled and hugged me.

Everyone except Granny, who remained seated on the floor, followed us out to the car repeatedly calling out, "Bye, John. Bye, John." Outside, a group of neighbours' children assembled and joined in the cacophony with yet more. "Bye, John." "Bye, John." "John! John! Goodbye! " And all waved enthusiastically as we reversed down the rough track to turn for home.

In those few moments I felt honoured. The Queen herself couldn't have had a better welcome. This was a taste of the kind of island life I wanted. Forget the tourist resorts with all the contrived pleasures they purported to offer. I wanted to mix with Fijian people, share in their lives, experience their culture, and learn from them.

That evening, Ray responded to my sentiments by organising an itinerary for me. In the morning I was to catch a bus to Beqa Lagoon, renowned for its soft coral, to do some diving, and return to spend the night with Ray and Wainese again. The day after, I would catch another bus and head north. It would drop me off at a remote bridge on the road round the island. I would be met there by a small boat and taken to a tiny island called Caqalai (pronounced Thang-al-eye) where I would stay for a few days with a Fijian family, the only regular inhabitants of the island. I would sleep in a bure, a traditional hut made of rough-hewn timber frames and woven palm leaves. There would be no running water or electricity: instead, there would be bucket showers and oil lamps for light at night. There would be beautiful beaches, shady palms, a beautiful lagoon to swim in, and friendly people who would cook traditional food for me and allow me to share in their way of life.

That night I lay in bed and wondered what adventures Fiji might have in store for me.

Chapter 15

SPECIAL OFFER

"Come in. Come in," called the woman as I poked my head through the open doorway of the shop. I had just spent an exciting day diving on reefs and wrecks in Beqa lagoon. Now, with time to spare before catching the bus back to Suva, I had been attracted by the traditional carvings on display and accepted her invitation to browse. Noticing I was alone, and no doubt realising that a woman was more likely to be tempted to spend money than a man, she asked, "Where is your wife?"

"I don't have a wife. She died some years ago."

"Oh, you poor man! But who takes care of you?"

"I take care of myself."

"Oh no! You can't take care of yourself. A man needs a woman to look after him. Do you not have a woman to look after you at all?" I shook my head in mock sorrow.

"Oh, but that is not good. You must have a woman to take care of you. Would you like me to find a good Fijian woman for you?"

"That sounds like a good idea," I laughed, wondering if I was about to be introduced to her attractive young assistant. Maybe the girl read my mind, for she made some excuse in

Fijian and left the shop hurriedly. The shopkeeper continued enthusiastically.

"I know just the woman for you. My aunty needs a husband."

This wasn't exactly what I had in mind. I'd barely been in there for sixty seconds and here she was talking of marriage! To aunty! Now, I don't want to offend aunties, but somehow the word lacks a certain appeal. This was becoming uncomfortable, but there was no stopping her.

"What do you do for a living?"

"I've retired."

"What did you do before you retired?"

"I was the head of a secondary school."

"Oh, that sounds perfect! You would be ideal for my aunty. She is an intelligent woman. She is a good cook, and will look after you well, take good care of you, and (she gave me a meaningful look) she will make you very happy." Then, in case I was too thick to realise what she was talking about (which of course I was), she moved in closer, the voice dropped a little, became confidential, "Fijian woman knows how to make good sex, keep a man happy in bed. You give me your name and address and telephone number and I will get my aunty to call you and you can meet her. Then you can try her for yourself."

Well, how was that for a deal? Test-drive the aunty? I had expected to experience cultural differences on my travels, but this was an eye-opener.

"But I'm backpacking. I'm staying with friends tonight, but I don't know where I'll be tomorrow." That should let me off the hook, I thought. I thought wrongly.

"No problem. I will give you my telephone number and you call me and I will arrange for my aunty to meet you here."

"But your aunty wouldn't want to meet an old guy like me," I protested. Funny how that phrase was sticking.

"You're not old!" she scolded. "Look at you. How old are you anyway?"

"I'm sixty."

"No! You don't look that old. I would have guessed no more than about forty-five." She looked me up and down and added, "Mmm… You look very fit. You've got a good body." She leaned towards me, touched my arm, and whispered, "I would like to have you for myself, but I have a husband and it would only complicate things. But you would be perfect for my aunty. She is forty-seven."

"But no Fijian woman would want to marry a Scotsman. It is cold in Scotland. She would be miserable."

"You don't need to take her to Scotland. You can live here. My family is important here. We own a lot of property. Family is very important in Fiji and if you marry my aunty, my family will take care of you. Give you both a house to live in. It's no problem." She certainly had all the answers. I think she saw me wilt under this relentless onslaught and moved in to clinch the deal.

"You must come back this way. Call me and I will arrange for my aunty to be here to meet you, then you take her out for dinner. Buy her a nice meal and maybe one or two drinks – just one or two, Fijian woman doesn't like any drunkenness – and then you bring her back here. Take her to the beach house over there and spend the night with her. You take her to bed and she give you good sex, make you very happy, and then you go to sleep. I will make breakfast for you in the morning."

But she wasn't finished yet. She reached into a basket and lifted out a bar of soap. "Here. I give you some of this soap."

She sniffed the wrapping. "Sandalwood. This is good for sex. Wash yourself all over with this first, then you smell good. We like that. Makes sex better."

Now who ever had a blind date set up so well? She had already thrust her telephone number into my hand. I was trembling, speechless. Only two days in Fiji and I had already been offered not just a dinner date with a lady, but a beach house, special pheromone enhancing soap to guarantee good sex, with complimentary breakfast thrown in, a wife, the use of a house for as long as I wanted - no need to suffer any more cold damp winters in Scotland - and an important Fijian family to look after me in my dotage. My destiny was all mapped out. What an offer! So what did I do? I looked at my watch.

"Oh, my bus will be here shortly. I must leave now."

"OK. But remember to come back this way. You need a good woman to look after you. No man should be living alone."

I bailed out and ran to the bus stop. Sitting in the bus on the way back to Suva I began to see the funny side of it all. Ray and Wainese had some friends round for a barbecue that evening and they all had a good laugh at my predicament.

"Well, you never know, the aunty might be a stunner," laughed Ray. "Don't be put off by the fact that she is forty-seven and still looking for a husband. A lot of Fijian women won't put up with the way some Fijian men treat them. European men are highly regarded here, and although there is an element of the good provider in all this, they are loyal and look after their men well. Aunty could be just what you need, John. Maybe it would be worth exploring this further."

Maybe. I still had the piece of paper with the phone number on it.

Chapter 16

IT'S AN ILL WIND

I t was an instinctive reaction. Well, what else would you do when three lanes of growling traffic suddenly roar away from the traffic lights while you are crossing the road in front of them?… Sprint!

Well, that was the intention, but it is not a good idea at 8 a.m. with a backpack on, when you haven't done your warm-up exercises. With a snap like a rubber band breaking, I felt a massive stab of pain, as if I had been chopped in the back of my leg by an axe. Instead of describing the graceful, propulsive, forward movement of an athlete, my left leg dragged, toes down, along the tarmac. I gasped and hopped like mad for the other side. Once there, I put my foot down and nearly collapsed. I couldn't walk.

I was about to catch the bus that would take me to Wandalice Bridge where I was to be picked up by boat and taken to Caqalai. If I went to a doctor now I would miss the bus. The boat would have had a wasted trip, and who knows what the doctor might say? They are always such spoilsports and want you to stop doing things you enjoy. The worst of the pain was deep inside the calf muscle and my thought was that if I had torn it, rest would almost certainly be the best thing… Forget the doctor… Might as well get on the bus. Climbing up the steps was agony. I flopped into the seat behind the driver and wondered how this would affect my subsequent travels.

The scenery along the coast road was vividly green, lush forests and fertile farmland interspersed with villages, and only the occasional small town. A long way from nowhere, the driver turned round and called, "Wandalice Bridge."

I stumbled off, and bearing my weight on one leg, slung my backpack on my shoulders. A dirt path led down to the water's edge. I regarded it with a lack of enthusiasm. Any stretch on the back of my leg sent an agonising pain into the depths of the calf muscle and the ankle itself was now swollen and intensely painful. Clambering down a steep path to the riverbank while carrying a backpack was not what my leg wanted at this time.

Once down, I dropped the backpack, sat on the bank, and leaned back against it. It was 10:30 a.m. - pick up time. There was no boat, no jetty; only silence, and a sluggish, muddy river with heavily wooded banks. I sat and looked at the trees. And waited. Ten minutes later I heard the sound of an outboard motor. A boat with three men and a boy appeared. It was coming down river. Wrong direction. It beached below the bridge and the crew began unloading sacks filled with clams and carried them to the roadside. I was getting worried in case I was in the wrong place and checked with them. They confirmed that the boat from Caqalai would arrive here – eventually.

A minibus stopped up at the roadside. The shellfish and some of the crew went aboard and it left. The others walked away to who knows where. I was alone with the river, and the trees, and the silence, again. I could only sit and wait, in pain. In the silence. Silence can be unnerving. I listened intently: only the odd crab scuttling about in the mud at the water's edge, the shrill cry of a kingfisher, and the rumble of an occasional vehicle on the bridge overhead. And more silence.

Here I was, a pensioner, crippled, about as far from home as it's possible to be on this planet, not quite knowing where I was supposed to be going and quite unable to go anywhere. What would my mother say if she could see me now? Funny how you think of your mother at a time like that. If the boat doesn't show up, what then? This was not a time for negative thoughts. Stay positive in the face of adversity. I could always hitch a lift and beg for a bed somewhere along the road. These were friendly people. Better still: I could telephone the shopkeeper at Beqa Lagoon and ask her to send Aunty out for me! Let her take care of me, feed me, wash me with sandalwood soap, and give me good sex, then I could go to sleep. But with a backpack to carry and only one serviceable leg, how do I find a telephone in this wilderness?

Fifty minutes had passed since I got off the bus. Was that the sound of a boat's engine? Coming up river too. The noise appeared to change direction several times - the river wound through mangrove swamps. At last it appeared. A young man in his early twenties was at the helm and a youth in his late teens sat in the bow. It headed in towards me.

"John?"

"Aye, that's me," I called back with some relief.

The helmsman jumped ashore and held out his hand. "I'm Mopsje. This is Scorese. Where are you from John? Give me your pack. Come aboard and take a seat. We have to go to the village for a few minutes."

I settled down on a pile of lifejackets and they disappeared along the road to the village. The boat was about 24 feet long and narrow in the beam, with a fibreglass hull. Powered by a 30 HP Yamaha outboard, its shallow draught and planing hull were well suited to the local conditions. The seas around this part of Fiji are sprinkled with lumps of coral lurking just below the surface. This boat could skim across the surface drawing only a few inches of water and beach anywhere.

Half an hour passed before the boys appeared again. They climbed aboard and stowed a bag of provisions and a large plastic box of ice cream. The engine roared into life, they cast off, and we turned and headed down river rapidly; bow rising, stern digging in, leaving a white, churning, V-shaped wake. Scorese tore open the lid of the box of ice cream and turned towards me.

"Do you like ice cream, John?" and offered me the box.

"What do I eat it with?" I asked.

He looked at me with surprise. "Fingers!" and made a scooping gesture. Of course! I dug two fingers in and took a genteel portion, about a teaspoonful. Mother had always insisted on good table manners. I must not be greedy.

"Oh, take more than that," he remonstrated. He then dug in his own fingers: four of them went in like an excavator bucket and scooped out a massive lump of ice cream which went straight into his mouth. Mopsje then bent forward and did the same. The box came back to me. Well… I did want to savour Fijian life after all. I dug in four fingers and scooped out a sizeable lump. I might as well get my share before this pair of gannets scoffed the lot! I gave up a few scoops later; their fingers were dipping into my territory and I had no way of knowing how clean they were. They carried on scooping ravenously until there was only a milky mush in the bottom, then lifted the box to their lips in turn and drank what was left. Two litres of ice cream devoured - mainly by them - in just a few minutes.

After several minutes winding through the mangroves, we cleared the river mouth and headed out to sea. Dotted around the lagoon, clumps of trees seemed to be growing right out of the sea, creating a rather surreal effect, like a mirage. These palms had grown from coconuts which had taken root on coral outcrops.

About forty-five minutes later, Mopsje pointed ahead and called out, "Caqalai." We swung round to the west side of the island and I looked at it approvingly. Covered in palms and other vegetation, it was fringed by white beaches. We motored slowly towards the beach and a few buildings became visible among the trees. This looked promising; straw huts, thatched roofs, shady groves among the trees, and a glorious beach with a sprinkling of bikini-clad bodies sunbathing on it. Not bad at all.

The boat grounded gently on the sand and I swung my legs over the side and slipped into the water. It was deliciously warm and clear. My left foot sank into the soft sand. I winced in pain, stumbling and grabbing the boat for support. A local girl in her mid-twenties came running down the beach towards me. "Bula! I'm Dauni. What have you done to your foot? Oh, you can't walk. Here, put your arm over my shoulder." She put her arm round my waist and held me tightly. "Hold on to me and I'll take you to your bure." Well, this wasn't so bad after all!

Clinging to each other, we limped along the path through the palms to my beach house. "Unfortunately your bure is furthest away," she apologised. There was no need for any apology. I would have been happy to walk round the entire island clinging to this girl.

Traditional bure. My Fijian home on the beach.

She took me in and sat me on the floor. I looked around my quarters. The only furniture was a bed, flowery patterned sheets covering a mattress laid on a rough-hewn frame with a mosquito net bundled above. A mat of woven, dried pandanus leaves covered the sand floor. Walls and roof were of tightly woven palm leaves tied to coarse wooden frames. Three walls had tiny window openings: no glass, only wooden flaps. The doorway faced out to the beach just a few steps away, with waves gently lapping on the shore. Ray had fixed me up nicely. It was idyllic

View from the door.

"Now, let me see your leg," she commanded. She began to massage my leg gently with my foot resting on the inside of her thigh and then murmured, "How does that feel?" There was no way I could give the girl an honest answer!

"That feels good," I muttered, wondering if she could hear my pulse beating.

"You'll need a massage every day. Would you like me to come and massage you until it gets better?"

"Yes, please." I tried not to sound too delirious. This was unbelievable. Here I was on a tropical paradise island with an attractive girl wanting to massage me every day. I hoped the leg wouldn't heal too soon. She carried on stroking me and looked up quizzically.

"Are you married?" I explained my circumstances.

"And do you have a girl friend?" I shook my head.

"Right. You need someone to look after you. Would you like me to take care of you?"

"Oh, that would be great."

"Okay. I will be your wife." Not another one!

"Eh, well, but I've got to go back to Scotland."

"That's okay. I would love to go to Scotland. When do we leave?"

I couldn't believe this. I'd only been in Fiji for three days and I'd had two offers of marriage already. This wiped out the memory of my failure to impress the ladies of Tahiti. But it was all a bit too hasty for me.

"Well… Marriage isn't something to leap into. In my culture we take some time about things like that."

"OK. But you still need me to look after you here. You rest and I'll come back again and massage you." She left to prepare lunch, leaving me in a daze.

I wondered what lay in store for me in the next few days, or weeks. I had no idea how long my leg would take to heal - and I wasn't really bothered either! Things were looking interesting.

It's an ill wind that blows nobody any good.

Chapter 17

IN THE MOOD FOR LOVE

A sound like a foghorn announced lunch was ready. Siggi, our seventeen year-old waiter, blew through a large triton shell each time food was being served. We ate in a communal dining area, an open-sided shelter with the kitchen at one end and a small bar selling soft drinks and snacks at the other.

I hobbled along with a stick to support me, but help was soon at hand. Epele, the ten year-old youngest son of the family, came towards me with a worried look and asked what was wrong with my leg. Then he gestured to put my arm over his shoulder and he would support me and together we limped along. He was a real star. I've never met a ten year-old with such charisma. When dancing, his confidence, sensuous movements, and lack of inhibition had five English girls drooling. He simply oozed sex-appeal. I found myself envious. Why couldn't nature spread it about a bit more?

The English girls were all mathematics graduates from Leeds University so we struck up an immediate rapport.

A couple of English lads, a Danish family of four, two American girls, and an Italian called Alberto with a limp from a broken ankle while playing football, were the other visitors.

The inhabitants of the island were Kanai, his wife Dubai, their six sons and one daughter, and an extended family of several cousins, aunts, and the odd friend who dropped in for a few days, weeks, months, or maybe even years to help out in return for food and lodging. This mobility appears to be quite normal. Hospitality is offered without question; drop in and you are treated as a member of the family. This made it confusing for visitors trying to get to know all the names and map out the relationships for they came and left the island freely. The indigenous population of the island varied between twenty and twenty-five.

This tiny island - a leisurely stroll round the entire shoreline only took about thirty minutes - was owned by the Methodist Church. Kanai managed it for the church as a small holiday resort, offering a relaxed and relatively primitive holiday experience quite distinct from the more commercialised tourist resorts on Viti Levu.

Each afternoon, visitors had the opportunity to learn traditional crafts such as basket weaving, making mats, carving kava cups, and making brooms. The natural resources for all of these came from the palm tree. It was a pleasant way to spend time, sitting in the shade of the trees, learning new skills, and socialising. Snorkelling in the lagoon and walking round the island were other popular pastimes, and at 4:30 p.m. when the afternoon work was done, the family and visitors engaged in a game of volleyball - a daily ritual. Age, like gender, was irrelevant; young and not so young, male and female, all played the game with enthusiasm and skill. Yet their competitiveness was tempered by a tolerance of the relative lack of ability and experience of their guests and this facilitated the bonding process between visitors and locals. Unfortunately, I could only watch.

I was a long way away from any doctor and the severity of the pain when any pressure was put on the leg caused difficulty in walking. Kanai asked me to lie down while he had a look at my leg. He examined me, then gave the boys some orders. "I have sent the boys into the bush to gather some healing leaves for you, John. We'll wrap them round your leg for a couple of days and that should help take away some of the pain. Bush medicine. We have our own remedies." I must have looked a bit sceptical for he smiled and added, "They do work."

When the boys returned, the leaves were layered round my leg and a bandage wrapped round them to keep them in place. Two days later it was removed. The leaves had become a soggy, green mess and my leg had a greenish tint to it. Kanai asked me to take a few steps. I did. The pain had eased; the swelling was down significantly. I could walk, with care. I was dancing every night too after that.

The boys provided musical entertainment while we dined each evening. Bill and Scorese played guitars, Mopsje played an improvised tea-chest one-string base and harmonised in vocals with Bill. Having learned I could play spoons, Siggi emerged from the kitchen each evening with a pair of dessert spoons, pulled a chair up beside the band, laid the spoons on it, and gave me a knowing smile. From then on I provided percussion. The girls from the kitchen and some of the boys invited guests to dance and this was where Epele demonstrated his talent. No girl ever refused to dance with him. His eight year-old sister, equally charming and always dressed beautifully for the evening entertainment, simply ignored my impediment, and with big, brown eyes looking into mine, asked, "John, you dance?" I danced. She was irresistible.

Most nights we joined the family for the traditional ritual of kava drinking in a vacant dormitory. Kava is made from the root of a shrub of the pepper family, cut up into small pieces, dried in the sun, and pounded into a fine powder. This is then placed in a muslin bag in the Kava bowl, a large basin-sized bowl carved from hardwood. Water is poured in and the bag is thoroughly soaked and squeezed until the water is a muddy, greyish colour. The resulting infusion is given a good stir and a communal cup made from a half coconut shell is used to serve it.

Making Kava. Looks like muddy water - tastes like it too.

This ritualistic activity is carried out with due observance of protocol. Everyone sat cross-legged on the floor - chairs were non-existent here apart from those in the dining room. On occasions when the local chief came over from Motoriki, the larger neighbouring island, he had to be served first, and he brought his own cup. The communal cup was filled from the bowl and the kava was then transferred into the chief's cup and placed deferentially on a mat in front of him. It was never handed to him directly. He clapped his hands once, then lifted the cup and said, "Bula." He drank, accompanied by three slow handclaps from the others. Kanai as head of the family came next, followed by any distinguished visitors from the other islands such as the local minister who came over on Sunday nights for an evening service. The guests were served next after which the cup circulated round the rest of the family. Unlike the bush beer drinking on Atiu, women were not excluded from this ceremony, although they were not in attendance as often as the men. They often still had work to do; washing clothes, preparing food, putting the children to bed.

Between rounds of the drink Kanai picked up his guitar and sang and the others joined in, often with skilful harmonies. Their musical ability was amazing. I seemed have been accorded special status, as a sort of representative of the guests, perhaps because of my seniority. Before each song, Kanai provided a few words of introduction always beginning, "John, this is a song about…." He never mentioned any others by name, or referred to us as a group, as though referring to me somehow included all the others. My accompaniment of the music on spoons was always acknowledged at the end of the song: "Thank you, John."

Kava is non-alcoholic, but it is a mild narcotic. It is said to induce a sense of relaxation. Certainly, as the evening progressed the locals became more laid back, often stretching full length on the floor as though ready to fall asleep, but always the next song had them sitting up and singing again. Some claim it has a numbing effect on the lips. It did nothing for me. Maybe I was so laid back by now that I couldn't lay back any further for I never experienced any effect at all, other than the taste. It looked like muddy water and tasted like it too. I noticed the chief and some of the ladies always popped a sweet into their mouths to kill the taste after each cupful. Perhaps the only effect it had on me was to ensure that I rose early each morning - it appeared to have a slight laxative effect.

With no plumbing on the islands, rainwater was gathered for cooking and washing. Several toilet cubicles were spaced around the community of huts. These were flush toilets, but you had to fill a bucket from a barrel of seawater standing outside the door and pour it into the lavatory bowl. Outside my bure, I used a large clamshell as a washbasin. Soaping my body all over and pouring a bucket of water over me served as a shower. It was primitive, but effective. Everyone appeared clean and tidy, and the clothes the family wore were always spotless.

The islanders all had the most beautiful, pearly white teeth. Curious about this, I asked Siggi if there was anything they ate that could account for their magnificent teeth. Aware of Fiji's notorious reputation for cannibalism until the latter half of the nineteenth century, he answered with a mischievous grin, "Yes. We eat people."

Each day followed a similar pattern; toilet, breakfast, sitting in the morning sun chatting with visitors or family, snorkelling or walking round the island. But not for me with my injury. I went back to my bure and lay on the bed and read. Then came lunch, more chat, afternoon activities such as learning traditional crafts, afternoon tea, volleyball, dinner, some dancing and kava. In spite of the lack of amenities we all enjoyed the rustic simplicity of life, and I never heard anyone complain - in fact several visitors extended their stay. I had never felt so relaxed in my life. Maybe the kava did have an effect after all.

One evening we had a sunset cruise on the lagoon. Two boats filled with visitors and several of the locals, with a few crates of beer and some kava (none of the locals drank alcohol), set off to cruise around the island and watch the sun set in a blaze of glory. The boys had their guitars and sang for us. We joined in when we could and danced. Epele danced on the cabin roof of one boat, presenting a seductive silhouette against the setting sun, his sinuous movements eliciting cheers of appreciation from the girls.

As darkness fell we beached beside a large bonfire where a barbecue had been prepared and sat on the beach eating dinner. The music started up again and everyone got up to dance. I tried, but it was too painful in the sand and I was forced to sit it out. However, the girls were there to comfort me. Dauni offered another leg massage while two other girls, Sherry and Fanga, lay on the sand on either side of me, stroking my hands and teasing me, much to the merriment of the boys.

"Oh John, my darling, will you take me back to Scotland with you?" said Sherry.

"No John, ignore her. Take me and I will be your wife and take care of you and massage you every night." said Dauni.

When I left to go to bed, the girls mischievously called out, "Don't forget, John. Leave the door of your bure open tonight and we will come and massage you later." That drew excited gasps and a few saucy comments from the boys.

I hobbled through the bushes to my bure, smiling to myself. I had earned a bit of street-cred with the lads, for although I was the oldest man on the island, I had three attractive girls in their early twenties fussing over me. I didn't mind the pain in my leg one little bit. Every cloud has its silver lining.

In expectation of the promised pleasures of massage, and whatever else, I washed all over with the sandalwood scented soap the shopkeeper had given me to make sure I had good sex with aunty. We'll see how this works, I thought. I shaved once more, humming the tune, *I'm in the mood for love*, and I didn't forget to leave the door of my bure open. I lay back on the bed, fresh and fragrant with the scent of sandalwood, in anticipation of a night of pleasure and passion.

No one came.

Chapter 18

STILL A TEACHER

People arrived or left the island almost every day. The five English girls - beautiful, exuberant, and intelligent - had been particularly good company, and I was sad to see them go. The Danish family had already gone, and the two lads and the American girls were also now leaving. In such a short time we had become friends, shared in so much fun and conversation, and enjoyed a unique sense of community on that tiny island. We all assembled at the beach and exchanged hugs, and the entire family gathered to sing a farewell song to their guests. It was a moving moment, and tears rolled down the girls' cheeks. As the final words of the song drifted out over the lagoon, Mopsje pulled the starting cord and the boat's engine roared into life. Everyone waved, called out their final goodbyes, as the boat reversed slowly away from the beach.

Dauni stood beside me, her arm draped over my shoulder. "John, wiggle your hips now," she commanded. In my few attempts at dancing I had been able to stand on one spot and wiggle my hips in something like the fashion of the Cook Islands girls. This had always been greeted by whoops of delight and, as she clapped out the beat, I swung into action. The ladies all whooped in rhythm, Dubai leading and calling out, "Swing those hips baby! Whoo, Whoo, Whoo." The sad faces of the girls on the boat turned to laughter and they called out too, "Yeah! Swing it John!" The engine revs picked up and they roared out into the lagoon, all laughing, waving, blowing kisses, and then they were gone.

It was a quiet and somewhat sombre lunch that day with only Alberto and me left. However, three more visitors arrived that afternoon: Aaron, from Vancouver, and from Australia, Susie and Heather, two attractive sisters still in their teens. Susie was about to start university; Heather still had another year at school. They were pretty quiet at first, but the island worked its magic on them, and by the time they left they were enjoying the banter and engaging in conversation.

Aaron and I clicked immediately. A sound engineer, he had given up work for a year to visit his girlfriend who was nursing in Sydney. His father lived in Nadi, so he was breaking the journey for a few days in Fiji. Despite the age gap, we quickly became very close friends. He was also very popular with the islanders who all called him endearingly, "Aa-roni."

Until he arrived, if a group of us had been sitting around talking and any of the islanders passed by, they always called out, "Morning John. Morning everyone."

Dauni, of course, had to make it more interesting by calling out, "Good morning John, my darling sweetheart. Morning everyone." This inevitably raised a few eyebrows and I was left embarrassed, trying to laugh it off, "Just Dauni having a wee joke." And not one of them believed it.

But Aaron had some special quality, and after a day or so the greetings became, "Morning John. Morning Aa-roni. Morning everyone." Why we should be greeted as individuals intrigued me. I observed everyone more closely. There was something distinctive about Aaron; about the way he watched, listened, and learned the skills we were taught, about the way he interacted with the islanders. He was quiet, respectful, empathetic; that special kind of person about whom you could say, 'he is one of us.' It was a good place for people watching - and learning.

Apart from the girls who cooked lunch, each Sunday the islanders went over to Motoriki for the church service. It proved to be an ecumenical event, with all the visitors joining in regardless of religious persuasion, and was part of the experience of living as the islanders lived, sharing in their daily lives. Dressed in our Sunday-best - long trousers and clean shirt - we arrived at the opposite shore, a flat muddy beach, and had to roll up our trouser legs and wade ashore. As we walked up the beach, Kanai came over to me. "The visitors will be welcomed to the church, John. Will you say a few words in reply?"

"Of course," I replied, then with a touch of panic, "but what should I say?"

"Just say what is in your heart," and he moved off to organise everyone.

The church was near the beach, and we all filed in and sat cross-legged on the floor. I looked around. Dark, smiling faces everywhere, all dressed in spotless white shirts and dresses, children all turning round to gaze at the pale-faced visitors. But what was I to say? I needed inspiration. I flicked open the Bible Dubai had passed to me, and my eye alighted on the last few verses of St Mark's gospel, chapter 3. Jesus had been preaching to the masses and, looking around those who sat about him, he said, "Here are my mother and my brothers. Whoever does the will of God is my brother and sister and mother."

Such had been the warmth of the welcome we had all experienced in Caqalai, so well had we been cared for - especially me with my injury - that these words more than adequately described my feelings about the people who had looked after us and, I felt sure, the visitors from Italy, Canada, and Australia would concur. I was comfortable speaking to the congregation. It was like addressing a school assembly again, and I could see by the reaction on the faces that my words had some effect. Eyes glowed, they smiled, and some heads nodded in silent acknowledgement. When I sat down again, Susie stroked my arm and whispered, "That was really nice, John." Heather nodded her agreement. Aaron, seated behind me, leaned forward and whispered, "Excellent, John. Thank you." Alberto smiled and winked. I heaved a sigh of relief.

When the service was over, the congregation remained seated as the minister came forward and led the visitors to the door. He placed me first, then all the others in line, and everyone leaving the church shook hands with us as they emerged. When the church had emptied, the minister came to me and said, "You spoke very well. What do you do in Scotland?"

I explained my former status as a headmaster and he smiled, "Ah, I was wondering if you had been a minister. The quotation from St Mark's gospel was so well chosen."

"Aye, it seemed appropriate," I agreed, but it must have been divine intervention that opened the Bible at exactly that page.

Another boatload of visitors arrived next morning. David and Kirsten were from New Zealand. David had just finished working on the film soundtrack of the second of the Lord Of The Rings trilogy. An excellent guitarist, he too joined the band, and we had some great jam sessions with his expertise enhancing the musical fare. One afternoon, when relatives from a neighbouring island arrived, we played to a large audience; a circle of dark, smiling faces with dazzling white teeth showing their appreciation. The spoons amused them and fascinated the kids. The boys sang an old song I remembered from my childhood, *You are My Sunshine*, which was having a revival in the islands at the time. I beckoned three wee boys to come and sit opposite me and I played the spoons on their knees. They loved it.

Kirsten was studying English at Wellington University. In my relatively immobile state, I enjoyed many hours in her company, discussing books and writing. Mark, a 37 year-old mathematics graduate from the USA, I recognised at once. I had seen him on Moorea. Although he had a PhD, he had forsaken academia for world travel and had taught English as a foreign language in Germany and China; another interesting character with a wealth of experience to share. Caqalai was proving to be a good place to be with an injured leg, my inability to engage in physical pursuits enabling me to exploit the opportunities for absorbing conversation.

Markus, a handsome Swedish professional golfer working the Australian and New Zealand circuit, was taking a break with his girlfriend, Anna, a lovely, blonde banker from Stockholm. Kurt, from Switzerland, and Eva, his East German girlfriend, had met as students at Heidelberg University. They all spoke English fluently and proved to be charming company. They were all thoughtful and intelligent, but it was Eva who excited my admiration most.

Having grown up in East Germany, Russian was the only foreign language she had been allowed to study at school. She had learned her first words of English only twelve weeks previously at the English Language School in Auckland, yet now she was speaking the language with an extensive vocabulary and familiarity with idiom. The very embodiment of determination, she had totally immersed herself in the language. She spoke only English, even with Kurt, refused even to think in German, and she now read only books written in English. She was the perfect student, stopping me to ask for an explanation of any unfamiliar word, phrase, or colloquialism I may have used, repeating it, and examining other words or phrases of similar meaning so she had some context within which to place it. I could only gaze in rapt admiration. This girl was every teacher's dream.

It made me feel shame at the little German I could speak after nearly six years working in that country, even though it had been thirty years previously. I could never sustain a conversation for any length of time, or to any depth, in German, yet all four of these Europeans were able to engage me for hours in serious, analytical discussions on a wide range of issues. My current lifestyle was regarded with some envy: they thought it close to perfection - apart from my single status. Even they thought I should have a soulmate, but I still had mixed feelings about that. Each meal time was similar to leading a tutorial with a group of bright students thirsting for knowledge, probing the mind of their tutor and his experience of the world, devouring, digesting, and debating his words and thoughts. I enjoyed that immensely. I had always revelled in tutorials; the sharing of ideas and experience leading to better understanding and mutual respect.

On the day Kurt and Eva were leaving the island, the boat had been delayed, and I had gone back to my bure to escape the blistering heat of the sun and had fallen asleep. I awoke an hour or so later, annoyed with myself, realising that by now they had probably gone and I hadn't been there to see them off. I went outside to wash my face in the clamshell.

"John! John!" I turned round and there was Eva running through the palms towards me, her arms outstretched, Kurt following in her wake.

"I've been looking everywhere for you, John. The boat is waiting, but I couldn't leave without saying goodbye to you." She threw her arms round me and gave me a lingering hug, murmuring in my ear, "John, you have taught me so much, and shared so much of your experience with me, and it has been wonderful to meet you. I hope you will find the happiness you deserve and someone special to share it with."

I was quite taken aback, humbled. "It's been a delight to meet you too, Eva. You are an amazing student, an example to us all. And you're no' a bad lad either, Kurt," I growled and shook his hand.

"We'll never forget you, John," he said warmly.

Eva wiped away a tear and murmured softly, "Goodbye John." And they both ran back to the boat.

I sat on the beach for a while, engulfed in the sadness that followed their departure, looking out over the lagoon's tranquil water shimmering in the mid-day sun. What magic this island had conjured up. What interesting people it had brought into my life, people with whom I had shared so much illuminating discussion. In these simple surroundings I was still learning. And they too had shown me that I was still a teacher, capable of inspiring and enabling young people.

Teaching is more than an occupation. It is truly a vocation, inescapably a way of life. The mantle of the teacher is more than a garment to be worn as the occasion demands: like a skin, it may grow and develop according to the environment, but it can never be shed.

Chapter 19

CUPID ON CAQALAI

S herry gave me lessons in the Fijian language. Intelligent, well spoken, with a degree in hospitality management, she was a friend of Dauni's and was spending a few weeks on the island to help out and offer staff training. A modern, independent sort of girl with a good education and excellent interpersonal skills, she didn't seem to me to be the kind who would be content to settle for the traditional way of life and I asked if, being in the tourism industry, she had any notions for travel herself.

"Oh yes, I would like to travel the world, to see other places and meet people from different countries and cultures."

"Well, if you ever consider coming to Scotland, I can promise you a good welcome," I assured her, thinking I was doing my bit for Scottish tourism. She looked on it differently.

"I would love to come to Scotland," she muttered longingly. "I could take care of you and be your wife." Why did everyone want to be my wife?

"Och, you girls should stop teasing me." I chided softly.

"We're not teasing," she murmured. I looked at her. Her face told me she meant it.

"But I have so much more travelling to do. I'm restless. I don't know when I'll ever settle down. And I'm so much older than you."

"Age doesn't matter," she countered. "And you need a woman to look after you." Did I really look so helpless?

"Mmm, maybe… but maybe not just yet."

That afternoon, some relatives came over from a neighbouring island and Dubai insisted that I come and sit with them in the shade of the trees. The only guest to receive such an invitation, I felt privileged as she introduced me to her relatives and friends. They regarded me politely, but with curiosity, and expressed their delight that I had travelled half-way round the world to visit this little island. Inevitably, the questions became more personal: my single status had become an unavoidable topic of conversation by now. They found it incomprehensible that I could exist without having a woman to look after me.

"Do you have *no one* to take care of you?" asked one of the men incredulously.

"No."

"Oh, *you* need a wife. That woman over there is available. She would make a good wife for you. She is a teacher too. Why don't you marry her?" That brought a chorus of approval from the others. The woman in question, a pleasant middle-aged lady, smiled at me through lowered eyelids.

I bowed my head in acknowledgement that I should be accorded such esteem as to be deemed so desirable to be offered yet another proposal of marriage - my fourth no less. I had started counting them by this time, my humility having been overwhelmed by the unavoidable recognition that the

Fijians were such good judges of character as to regard me as a significant prize. But humility fought back and regained supremacy. This was a time to exercise the arts of old-fashioned, gentlemanly diplomacy.

"I am sure that such a charming lady must have a queue of far more attractive suitors to chose from. Perhaps an old man like me would only prove to be a disappointment."

"How old are you?" The man asked. That allowed the conversation to change to safer ground. I had diverted the talk away from matrimony.

"How old are you?" was always one of the first questions the kids asked every visitor. Our ages were then often used as an appendage when they were rehearsing our names, as they often did when we sat round the table. "Aa-roni, twenty-seven; Alberto, forty-four; Anna, twenty-four; Markoos, twenty-nine; John - seexty!" The way they giggled at my age, I might have been Methuselah! The next question was "When is your birthday?" My birthday was coming on the following Monday so they practised, "John, Seex-one, Seexty-one!" They laughed.

"Hey, I don't feel that old! I only feel like John, one-six."

"John, one-seex? Seexteen? Ha Ha Ha!" And they all fell about laughing again. It wasn't meant to be *that* funny.

I have never been one for celebrating birthdays. It had always been just another day, not a milestone of any significance, a mere reference point in relation to the date when, released from the burden of professional responsibilities, I could live the life of a world-wide wanderer. I was now a piece of human flotsam on the oceans of the world, carried where the tide of fortune would take me. I gave it no more thought.

The kids had other ideas. On Monday evening as dinner drew to a close the islanders appeared, all beautifully dressed, wearing flowers in their hair. The kitchen door opened and Siggi, with his usual dazzling, cannibal-inspired smile, came forward bearing a platter with a birthday cake and a large knife. The boys in the band struck a chord and the entire assembly broke into song: "Happy Birthday to You." The cake was laid before me, and on it was written: JOHN - HAPPY BIRTHDAY - SWEET 16!

I offered a few words of thanks for their kindness, the music started, and we all danced. We played some silly games where we had to dance with balloons between our bodies or transfer oranges held under our chins from one to the other, and of course I had to "Swing those hips baby!" It was all good fun. But two were missing. Sherry had a day off to visit the mainland and Dauni was also missing. I wondered if I had offended her.

I still had Fanga to dance with. Fanga managed the accounts. A tall, slim, girl of Polynesian ethnicity - the others were predominantly Melanesian - she moved with the elegant, feline grace of a panther and when dancing demonstrated that easy flow of rhythmic sensuality accompanied by a serene smile that was characteristic of her race. We spent some time talking between dances. She was a gentle girl; quieter, more subtle than the others, but with a hint of a mischievous smile she asked me where I had learned to dance 'like that.' I explained my enjoyment of Polynesian culture, especially dance, and how I had learned a little in the Cook Islands. She murmured, "You dance very well." And with a sideways look, she suddenly asked, "What kind of soap do you use?"

I was taken aback. "Why?" I had a quick sniff at my armpits. "Do I smell bad?"

She laughed. "Oh no! You smell very nice. I just wondered what kind of soap you use. It smells like sandalwood."

Of course! It was the soap the shopkeeper had given me to make sure I had good sex with aunty. Maybe it was working its magic after all.

"Ah, there is a story attached to that," I said, and told her of the shopkeeper offering me her aunty. She howled with laughter - but *she* didn't ask me to marry her.

The following day, Sherry returned to the island, and after lunch she and Dauni joined me. Sherry asked if I had enjoyed the party. I expressed my sorrow that she had been unable to attend, and also that Dauni had stayed away. Dauni immediately apologised explaining that with Sherry being away all day she had all the cooking to do by herself and had fallen asleep after preparing dinner.

"You fell asleep? How could you fall asleep knowing that your 'darling sweetheart's' birthday party was due? Oh well, now I know how little I mean to you?"

"Oh, that's unfair! Who do you think stood for hours lovingly baking that cake for you? It's no wonder I felt tired." Her protest shamed me. It was time for some old-fashioned gentlemanly diplomacy again. I bent down on one knee and kissed the back of her hand.

"Please forgive me for being so insensitive. I would like to thank you, sincerely."

She smiled graciously. "I accept your apology."

I changed to safer topics of conversation and later asked them for the name of a CD which they often played in the kitchen as they worked. It contained many of the songs sung by the boys at dinner. "I would like to buy a copy so that when I go back to Scotland I can play it to remind me of Fiji," I said.

"It would be better if you would take a Fijian wife home with you, then you wouldn't need to be reminded of Fiji," Dauni retorted. These girls don't give up easily.

"Ah, but how do I chose between two such attractive girls?" I protested.

"Simple," she said. "Just pick one." I looked at the two dark, smiling faces with flashing eyes. If only it were that simple.

There was no escaping the fact that marriage was in the air. Paul and Sheryl, a young English couple who arrived shortly before Christmas, will remember Caqalai for the rest of their lives. It was there on the beach, early on Christmas morning before Sheryl had risen, that Paul scratched out a message in the sand in the Fijian language. He had involved me in his plan as his consultant, knowing that Sherry had taught me some of the most important words and phrases. When Sheryl came out for an early morning swim she looked at the message in bewilderment. "What does it say?"

Paul took her hand and got down on one knee. "It says, 'I love you. Will you be my wife?'"

Tears of joy filled her eyes, and she threw her arms around him. "Yes! Of course I will."

Sherry's teaching had proved effective, even if not quite in the way she had planned, but Cupid had found work on Caqalai at last – and he wasn't finished yet.

After dinner, everyone met for the kava drinking ceremony. As people went off to bed and the crowd thinned out, I noticed Susie gradually moving closer to Ben, one of the local boys, who was sitting in a corner grinding kava with mortar and pestle. With his good looks and dazzling rakish smile, I reckoned things were looking promising for him. I went off to bed too.

Before I left Scotland I had visited an old friend, my former doctor, who had worked in Fiji for some years. Aware of the possibility of picking up some tropical disease, I knew he could give me expert advice, based on first hand experience. "Stewart, I'm going to Fiji. What are the health risks, and what can I do for protection?" His reply took me by surprise.

"Gonorrhea. And you know what the protection against that is."

"Abstinence."

"That's not what I had in mind," he retorted.

"Well, bearing in mind my age and track record I wouldn't have thought that likely," I protested.

"Don't be so sure. Age is irrelevant. Attitudes to sex are very different there. You may not go out looking for it, but it may well come looking for you, and you might find it hard to resist. Take a supply of condoms anyway."

So I did, just in case I might be overpowered some dark night by a lusty maiden who wouldn't take no for an answer. However, the condoms were still lying unused in my backpack - and it didn't look as though they would be needed - but Cupid still had some magic to conjure up that night.

I was in a deep sleep when a voice broke through, calling, "John. John. Wake up!" Through the haze of my mosquito net I could just make out a dark human form silhouetted against the lighter darkness of the open doorway. Ever the optimist, I was still remembering to leave the door of my bure open at night. Was this my luck changing at last? Who could it be? Dauni? Sherry? Fanga? I fumbled under my pillow for my small torch and flicked the switch. My fantasy dissipated with the speed of light. It was only Ben, naked except for a skimpy pair of briefs.

"What's the matter?" I mumbled.

"John, could you give me a condom?" He hissed.

"Eh? Och aye, sure," I reached down for my pack, pulled one out, and passed it to him.

"Thanks, John." And he sprinted off into the darkness.

I lay back on my bed and began to laugh, remembering Stewart's words. I'd carried these condoms half-way round the world, half-hoping that I might share some torrid nights of passion with a nubile, sun-bronzed maiden under the swaying palms of an idyllic Pacific island, and here I was supplying a testosterone-laden young buck from Fiji with the means of satiating the erotic desires of the nubile maidenhood of Australia. It was not quite as Stewart had predicted.

Then I became intrigued. Why did Ben come to me for one? The young guys were surely a more likely prospect. Maybe I had a bit of street-cred here right enough. It's all about perception, not so much what you do, as what people imagine of you. But I had done nothing. Teasing was all I got! I stopped laughing and began to bash my head in anguish against the pillow. Why should the young ones have all the fun?

I wasn't too old - yet!

Chapter 20

MAYBE SOME DAY

I t was quite unlike any other Christmas. The entire population of the island, two boat-loads of relatives who had come from neighbouring islands to spend a few days, and all the visitors assembled in the dormitory for a church service on Christmas morning. A minister had come over from the mainland; a rotund, jovial fellow who spoke with such sincerity and conviction that, even though it was all in a foreign tongue, it was impossible not to feel a sense of inspiration in his message.

When his sermon was over, Dubai indicated to me that I was expected to speak. With no time for preparation, the words, 'Do unto others as you would have them do unto you,' and 'Love thy neighbour' flashed into my mind.' They seemed appropriate to how well treated we had all been on this lovely wee island, and I expressed my thanks once again for the wonderful hospitality we had received. At the end of the service several of the islanders came to me to thank me for my words, both Sherry and Dauni hugged me, and the minister engaged me in conversation for some time afterwards.

A feast was served in the dining area. Roast pork, chicken, tuna, shark, barracuda, and all sorts of fruit and vegetables were laid out for almost fifty people. How the women had worked this miracle with such limited facilities over the last few days defied understanding. It was a feast fit for a king. Visitors and relatives were served first. The island women worked in the kitchen while Kanai and the boys served the food. Only after we had eaten our fill would they sit down and eat.

Afterwards we all drifted off for a siesta, or a leisurely swim. I lay on my back in the warm, shallow water reflecting on how different Christmas would be in Lochcarron. The village would still be asleep, perhaps with snow silently falling outside, trees clothed in white glittering against the night sky - more likely it would be raining!

Snow was an unknown weather phenomenon in this part of the world, yet here they still embraced all the traditions of a European Christmas, decorating the dining room with a tree, and lights, and decorations. The kitchen girls wore red Santa Claus hats trimmed with white fur, and worked happily at their labours, singing and dancing to the sound of Christmas carols. It all seemed rather incongruous.

I had no regrets about being away from home at Christmas; the cynical commercial exploitation, the wasteful expenditure lavished on presents, many of which would soon be discarded… all of that annoyed me. The people here had little more than a roof over their heads, shared a room with three of four other people, owned few personal possessions, yet they gave so much - not in any material sense, but in friendship and hospitality.

I once asked Sherry why, with so little, everyone seemed so happy on this island. "We have no need of material things," she replied. "We live with God."

And they did. The entire family assembled each morning and evening for prayers led by Kanai, and the sound of hymns, sung with passion, could be heard drifting through the trees from their quarters.

We regard Christmas as a time for families to be together; that's fine, but for me the death of my wife left an immense void. We were not all together as a family, and never would be again. Her premature death had denied her the opportunity to see her grandchildren growing up, and I grieved that she had not been able to share in the pleasure they gave me. For me, Christmas at home seemed only to emphasise that sense of loss. It had become a depressing time of year, and I wanted to be away from it all.

What was so refreshing for me now was to be with people I had only met a few days previously. In our self-chosen exile, we had been drawn together in a genuine spirit of goodwill. There wasn't a shop in sight, no TV with glitzy, packaged, self-proclaimed merriment, no radio, no newspapers, no rain, no snow, no biting frost, no burst water pipes - only the spirit of Christmas with its plea for goodwill towards all. That was evident in the example of the islanders who had embraced us with such affection. Its message of hope for the future lay in the potential of these bright, cheerful, young travellers who had filled me with optimism. I had no regrets about being here. It had been an uplifting experience.

Most of the pain and swelling in my leg had subsided and, although still unable to raise my heel, I was able to hobble along with a flat-footed, limping gait. My time had now come to leave the island. After dinner on my last night, the boys sang all the usual songs, but the final one was special, moving, haunting, as in harmony they sang, "I'm going back to my homeland, maybe some day I'll come back again…" Yes, maybe some day I would come back to this little bit of paradise so indelibly fixed in my memory.

Alberto, Paul and Sheryl, and the portly minister were also leaving with me in the morning. The whole family and all the visiting relatives turned out to say farewell. Their departure song in Fijian, so often heard before, was never so moving as now. By the time they finished, I was struggling with my emotions. Kanai and the boys all filed past, shaking hands with me, muttering sad farewells. Dubai, my Fijian 'mother,' and all the ladies followed and hugged me.

As Dauni held me close, she whispered in my ear, "Please come back, John."

"Aye, I will," I murmured.

I climbed on to the boat and Kanai fired up the engine. Everyone ashore started waving, and I waved back. Tears began to roll down my cheek. Then Dubai did it again: "Hey, John! Swing those hips, baby!" She started clapping her hands and whooping, and the others all joined in. I got the arms going, the body snaked sensuously, the hips made like a washing machine, and a great cheer broke out ashore.

Dubai called out to Kanai and he turned back. She had forgotten something. As the boat went in close she ran into the water with a bucket and a bag of flour, tipped the flour over the minister's head, and then poured half a bucket of sea water over him. Everyone erupted in fits of laughter. The poor man looked like a snowman, but took it all in good part. Can you imagine that happening to a minister in Scotland?

As we turned out again, she started the clapping and whooping once more, "Swing it John! Swing those hips, baby!" And I was into the aerobics again. About 100 metres out I stopped. The boat was called back in again.

"What is it this time?" I asked Kanai.

He grinned. "They want you to do another encore."

I swung those hips once more, and this time we were finally allowed to leave. They stood there on the beach, all waving, diminishing in size, never stopping until we moved round the island and they were at last out of sight.

As we left Caqalai behind, I could still hear the voices of Mopsje and Bill, harmonising sweetly in their song, 'Maybe some day, I'll come back again.' A heavy shower of rain swept across the lagoon obliterating the island from view. A curtain had at last been drawn on that idyllic stage on which so many dramas had been enacted, on which romance had flourished and, for some, had blossomed.

But I was still single - and celibate.

Chapter 21

MELBOURNE

After life on a Fijian island with a population of twenty-five, Melbourne was a bit of a shock to the system. I gazed at tall buildings and wide streets thronging with people, shops, trams, buses. I was back in the 21st century - and not too comfortable with it. I caught a tram to the youth hostel, bought some food, had supper, and went to bed longing for the soft lapping of the waves outside my door, the gentle glow of an oil lamp, and the rustle of the breeze among the palms. I needed a few days to acclimatise.

I'm not a city person, but Melbourne is not too bad, and I tolerated it for a couple of days. Its compact downtown area is suggestive of the intimacy of a big town rather than a city with the colourful Victoria Market bustling with people, bright shop fronts, well tended gardens along the riverside, and restaurants to match the tastes of the cosmopolitan mix of people on its streets. Each evening I dined out, sitting at a table on the pavement watching the world walk past; Orientals, small in stature, but so neatly proportioned, bulky Australians, Asians, Europeans, but not a single aboriginal did I see anywhere in the state of Victoria. Melbourne has a 'British' feel to it. There's even a Scots Kirk. After attending the church service there, I was invited to the church hall for a cup of tea. "Which part of Scotland are you from?" asked the lady who served me.

"Och, you'll probably never have heard of it. I live a wee village in the highlands called Lochcarron."

"Oh, I've heard of it alright," she replied. "My great grandparents were married in Lochcarron Church. Hey Willie," she called to her husband, "come and meet John. He's from Lochcarron." And so I was welcomed into the brotherhood of the kirk.

Melbourne's eclectic architecture intrigued me. A sprinkling of venerable late 19th and early 20th century buildings sit among a mix of pre-war art deco, post-war austere functional, and elegant tower blocks of the late 20th century. A mere infant compared to many European cities, it is a thrusting upstart, challenging concepts of visual harmony and style. A walk through the rectangular array of streets in the city centre led me to the river from where this jumble of structures can best be viewed.

There, on the riverbank, was the most arresting sight of all, the Ian Potter Centre, which houses the Australian part of the art collection of the National Gallery of Victoria. It is, frankly, provocative. A bizarre, angular building, its exterior appearance was initially shocking. It looked like something knocked up by ham-fisted navvies, working without a square or plumb line, from the reconstituted sections of the hull of a battleship painted in the grotesque grey, blue, and black hues of wartime camouflage. Yet inside it was marvellous. I'm not much of an art gallery person, but this one offered an absorbing selection of works of art, and its recognition of the work of living artists was commendable. I found the work of the aboriginal painters and sculptors particularly captivating.

I sat outside later, having a drink in the sunshine, and looked askance at this weird building. Words such as 'beautiful', 'elegant', 'graceful' were never coined for this mishmash. What kind of a mind could have conceived such a creation? What kind of statement was the architect trying to make - and why? I recalled then a conversation with Cindy Jones, a former pupil, now an art teacher, who was appalled at my lack of appreciation of art. "Think of a work of art as a statement. To understand it requires participation, some effort on your part. You have to open a book, read, and think about what you have read; and it may take several hours to appreciate what the author is trying to say. Give the same consideration to a painting or sculpture. Stand back and let your mind work on it."

The Ian Potter Centre

So I did. I gazed at this building in wonder and the more I gazed, the more the wonder grew. It was like looking at a woman whose wildly eccentric appearance may not conform to conventional concepts of physical beauty yet, as your acquaintance grows, you come to realise she has a caring nature, a captivating smile, and an interesting personality. Her outward appearance, in contrast to her subtle inner beauty, is challenging your preconceptions, compelling your curiosity to look beyond the superficial to find the essence of the real being, and is forcing you to examine your own sense of who you are. As I sat there cogitating, it dawned on me that I was having an educational experience. This building was making me think, making me examine myself, and my attitudes – and was that, after all, not partly why I was travelling the world? It was provoking me to look at myself critically, to see myself as others saw me, and consider what was lacking in me - or in my life.

As a teacher I had encouraged my students to think critically, examine perceived wisdom, be prepared to step outside the known parameters, and challenge the status quo. This remarkable structure had worked its magic on me. It has left an imprint as the most enduring image of Melbourne. It didn't generate the instant emotional response of the Sydney Opera House – surely the most remarkable piece of architecture of the 20th century - but I have no doubt that the Ian Potter Centre of the Victoria National Art Gallery will establish itself as another Australian architectural icon. It seemed an appropriate metaphor for that sometimes shocking, but nevertheless endearing, characteristic of the Aussies - they just don't give a damn for convention.

Sydney Harbour Bridge and Opera House.

Sitting there, watching the people stroll past, I could see it in the way they dressed - especially the men. I don't know what they feed on, but there are a lot of big guys in Australia. By comparison, I felt quite undernourished and scrawny. They were not just tall, but big-boned and bulky, tending towards being overweight, heavy limbed, and cumbersome. Many of them don't enhance their appearance by the way they dress: almost uniformly it seems, in baseball caps, shorts that drooped to well below knee level, and sleeveless T shirts exposing armpits that were hairier than a wombat's belly.

This unparalleled display of sartorial inelegance was complemented by what I began to recognise as the Victoria Walk, a peculiar amble characteristic of the male of the species *Homo Sapiens Victoriae*. They accentuate their glaikitness (a most aptly descriptive Scottish word) by slouching. The shoulders droop forward (never a good old-fashioned square set of shoulders in sight here), arms hang like redundant appendages from their sockets, hands dangle with knuckles facing forwards, open palmed, with the fingers hanging limp and as useless as the rest of the arm. Imagine a man nailed to the wall, hanging from a point somewhere between the shoulder blades forcing everything to droop and sag forward, and you have the picture.

And the legs get only marginally more deployment than the arms. When walking, the feet aren't lifted off the ground as the rest of the world walks, rising on ball of the foot, swinging the foot forward, then heel down. Here the foot is merely raised a few millimetres, dragged forward and scuffed down again in flat-footed fashion. It presents a most un-athletic, unintelligent looking, knuckle-dragging aspect – and this in a land renowned for its worship of sport.

Had this only been observed among spotty-faced adolescents I would have thought nothing of it, but here it was characteristic of all ages. This struck me as strange in such a fine city where I expected to see some slick dressing, but this is Australia where things happen that don't elsewhere. Not everyone looked like this of course - there were exceptions. They were probably visitors.

However, as with the Art Gallery, the visual aspect camouflaged much of what lay behind the façade. It was hard not to like the Australians. They displayed warmth and rough-hewn friendliness, and have a propensity in conversation for conjuring up the most delightfully colourful and descriptive phrases. Like the Americans, they have adapted the English language and shaped it to reflect their own image: brash, colourful, larger than life, and downright irreverent.

The bus drivers all used PA systems to keep travellers informed, but with some friendly wisecracking as well:

"Welcome aboard ladies and gentlemen. Are you all happy this morning?" Now wasn't that nice?

"Yes!" we all called back.

"Good. Well, you lot sound a helluva lot cheerier then the shower of miserable bastards I had on board yesterday." I almost choked. He would have been sacked for that in the UK.

One hot afternoon, I was standing with another backpacker at a bar, waiting for a cool beer to be poured. A local red-neck, wearing a Crocodile Dundee-style hat, came up to the bar and, without the courtesy of waiting his turn, called out to the barmaid, "Pour me a Foster's Sue."

The barmaid raised her eyes from the pump and retorted, "You'll have to wait till I've finished serving these two gentlemen."

He turned. A pair of ice-blue eyes set in a wrinkled, tanned-leather face regarded us with some bemusement. "Gentlemen? In this bloody place? They must be lost."

At a New Year's Day race meeting, the commentator announced over the PA system in that characteristically tense, earnest voice reserved for the line-up at the start, "They're all in now and they're under starter's orders..." As the horses burst from the traps, he exuberantly proclaimed, "And it's Royal Flush in the lead! Jeez, he's off faster than a bride's nightie!" Towards the end of the race, when the horse was coming down the home straight so far ahead of the rest of the field that there was nothing left to comment on, "And with one furlong to go, it's Royal Flush ahead by ten lengths, so if you put your money on him you might as well go to the bar now and celebrate."

I had little interest in the races, but I loved the commentary.

Cities can be among the loneliest places on earth as people go about their own business ignoring each other, and Melbourne suffers from this as much as anywhere else. No cheery greetings of "Bula" or "Kia Orana" from complete strangers here. Even in the hostel the attitudes were different. It was a different class of people. The Australian cricket team was in the process of humiliating - yet again - the England cricket team, and the hostel was filled with supporters of each side. One of the sad trends in this peculiar game, a sport once reputedly synonymous with gentlemanly behaviour (I can't speak with any authority on this, never having attained the status of either a gentleman or a cricketer), has been an increase in loutish behaviour on and of the field.

Now why anyone should wish even to cross the road to view anything so dull as a cricket match is beyond my comprehension, yet here were hordes of beer-bellied, loud-mouthed Englishmen, appropriately labelled the Barmy Army, who had travelled half-way round the world to watch their team receive a drubbing from more beer-bellied, loud-mouthed Aussies masquerading as cricketers. Crude verbal exchanges between at least one Aussie player and the Barmy Army had reached such a pitch in Melbourne that it was rated the most important news item on TV and in the newspapers. Maybe it would have been overlooked in Sydney where such behaviour is normal, but Melbourne is perhaps the most genteel of all Australian cities.

I had never seen or heard anyone, of any nationality, behave offensively in a hostel until then. The loutish, foul-mouthed behaviour continued even there. I was incensed by one guy leaning back on a chair with his feet, in grubby sweat-stained trainers, resting on a table used for dining. I decided to try telepathy to see if I could alter his behaviour - I had used it often as a teacher. I fixed my eye on him and concentrated hard. Somehow it caught his attention. My eye moved marginally and focussed on his feet. And the feet came off the table. Really, it worked. These guys weren't threatening anyone - they were just boorish.

Sleeping opposite me in the dorm was one grossly overweight, shaven headed, beer-swilling, amorphous mass who, after drowning his sorrows each night with the lads (and a game of cricket goes on for at least three days so he had plenty of sorrows to drown), grunted, snorted, sniffled, dribbled, belched, and farted continuously in his sleep. Having expelled all residual bodily gases and juices through his various orifices, on wakening he was quite pleasant.

The other backpackers made it clear that they had their own agenda - and mixing with a stranger wasn't on it. The only guy who was prepared to engage in conversation was Harry, a genial 78 year-old Queenslander, who told me he came to Melbourne for three weeks every year in the height of summer to escape the oppressive humidity in Brisbane. It seemed odd to me that he should want to exchange one large city for another for three weeks. Why not go to a pleasant, airy seaside resort? Did he have friends or relatives in the area to visit?

"No. I don't know anyone here. I buy one of these runabout tickets for the transport system. They're great value. You can use them on the trams, buses, or trains and go anywhere within the city transport limits. So every day I take a tram to the station, jump on a train or bus and see where it takes me, have some lunch and take the train or bus back. Most days I have no idea where I am going, but I get all over the city that way and see the suburbs."

Now that was an attraction that had escaped my notice!

He continued: "Even found myself right out at Applecross Beach the other day. Beautiful it was, and I had an ice cream there. Then I managed to get a train that took a different route back to Pitt Street, so that was a bonus. I had a great time. You should try it."

And he was serious. I enjoy travelling by rail, but the prospect of sitting all day in a train watching the backyards of the suburbs of Melbourne flash past for three whole weeks, was not high on my list of priorities. However, it was interesting enough for Harry to come back each year for more. It seemed absurd to me, but he enjoyed himself - and that's what mattered. He was a real gentleman.

Two days in Melbourne was enough for me. I took a train to Warragul, a small town about 60 miles to the southeast of the city to visit Helen, a girl I had taught in Germany. We had become re-acquainted through the internet, and on learning that I planned a visit to Oz, she had insisted that I call on her. I hadn't seen her since 1972.

And on the way I saw the suburbs of Melbourne from the train. Harry would have been pleased.

Chapter 22

THE VICTORIANS

"Mr McMillan!" Helen's cry greeted me as I stepped out of the railway station. She hugged me. I had wondered how this reunion with an ex-pupil from thirty years ago would work out, but based on our email correspondence, I felt optimistic. Of the thousands of pupils a teacher encounters, some are remembered for their outstanding ability, some for mischievous behaviour, and others because of their personality. Helen was in the latter category: vivacious, effervescent and chatty, she was a girl who always managed to get the last word. Now in her mid-forties, she hadn't changed in that respect.

The time lapse since we'd last swapped banter was irrelevant. We took up again as though we had parted only the day before, and three decades of gossip consumed the next three days. Her husband, Graeme, with his cheerful and jocular manner, ensured that there was no discomfort in fitting into this household.

Helen was the first of three ex-pupils I had been invited to visit. I had never regarded this as odd, yet so many people I had met on my travels had expressed surprise.

"You mean an ex-pupil actually wants to see you again? Can't think of any of my old teachers I would invite to stay with me."

Living in small communities in Scotland, I was accustomed to meeting pupils and ex-pupils socially. Some had invited me to their weddings, and in later years I taught their children too. It hadn't appeared odd to me that I should be invited to stay with ex-pupils on my travels, and I was looking forward immensely to meeting up later with Andrew in Sydney, and Cecily in Queensland.

But first, my plan was to explore the state of Victoria and do some diving. Graeme and Helen offered me the use of their 20 year-old Volvo to give me more flexibility than the limited public transport system would allow, and with automatic transmission my injured leg would have no work to do. I accepted their offer with gratitude.

Much of Victoria's rural landscape is similar to that of the UK, with cattle and horses grazing in fields fringed by hedgerows. I was on my way to Sorrento, one of the many holiday resorts along the coast of Port Philip Bay, Melbourne's summer playground. Now, at the height of the school holidays, it was jam-packed with holidaymakers, most of whom flocked to the campsites bordering the shoreline. In my youth, camping was something you did when hiking or kayaking, finding a spot by a stream where you could pitch a small tent for the night and cook dinner over a fire, or on a stove. This was different, a strip of coastline on which thousands had descended like locusts. It was clothed with caravans, chalets, tents, cars, bicycles and trucks, all within touching distance of each other. So grossly overcrowded were these campsites, they would have been condemned as a breach of human rights had they been refugee camps. The absurdity of it appealed to me. It was a reversal of what I thought was the essence of camping: peace and quiet to commune with nature, some personal space, and some privacy far from the maddening crowd.

Here was population density on a third world scale, and most of it had come from Melbourne, (just an hour's drive away), where they had air-conditioned bungalows with a quarter acre of leafy land around them offering at least a measure of privacy. Yet they swapped all that for concentration camp conditions, with their neighbours within arm's reach. It shows how sociable the Australians are!

It was not my ideal sort of place, but I'd heard the diving was good and I booked a diving trip at Portsea, a village at the mouth of the bay. They are quite proud to tell you that it was here in 1967 that Harold Holt, the Australian Prime Minister at the time, rashly plunged into the sea for a swim - and a few seconds later disappeared abruptly within yards of the shore. Maybe it was a shark that took him, or maybe he just got sucked under by one of the notorious tide-rips that are common here, but no trace of him was ever found. They built a fitting memorial to him in Melbourne - a swimming pool. The Aussies have a dark sense of humour.

The area just outside this almost landlocked bay is littered with wrecks, but with spring tides and a fresh breeze whipping up a lively sea, diving there was ruled out so we dived within the more sheltered water of Port Philip Bay. Even there we could only dive at slack water as the tidal currents were very strong. After the tropical temperatures of the seas around the Cook Islands and Fiji, I expected the south coast of Australia to be a bit cooler - but this was as cold as the sea in Scotland. Even wearing a thick wet suit, I was gasping. However, the body soon acclimatised and I was rewarded with the exploration of some colourful sponge gardens.

The best bit was swimming with a pack of seals. Before we entered the water the skipper told us, "Don't be afraid. They like company. When you get in the water just behave as if you were bloody daft - that shouldn't be too much of a problem for you lot. Spin yourself around, dive, turn somersaults, blow bubbles, and you'll find they'll imitate your actions. And just a word of warning to those of you who've already pissed in your wet suit – bull seals are sexually aroused by the scent of urine. There's no point in trying to deny it, we'll soon see who you are." No amorous approaches were made to me. Honest.

Basking on a man-made structure in the bay, the seals' curiosity was intense as we prepared to enter the water. As we approached, they plunged in too, diving with us, holding themselves suspended vertically - head down, tail up - peering at us with endearingly beautiful eyes, spiralling around us with joyful exuberance. They were as playful as puppies. It was a delightful experience.

That evening I received an email from Cecily. Her son and daughter from her first marriage, both in their late teens, were living just a few miles away with their father and she was really keen that they should meet me. I agreed to meet them next morning and have lunch with them. I was delighted that Cecily should want to meet me again, but that she should be so keen that her offspring - now young adults - should also meet me, enhanced the compliment.

I wondered how they would feel about this: two teenagers having been cajoled by a mother into meeting her old teacher didn't sound to me like the ideal recipe for a fun outing for them. I needn't have worried. I felt instantly at ease in their company and the conversation never flagged. At one point I had turned from speaking to Adam to face Tobi and gasped. Her elbow rested on the table, her chin was cupped in her hand as she listened, her eyes intent on me. It was the eyes that gripped me: they were the eyes of her mother thirty years ago. On leaving, Adam shook my hand and said, "I can see why Mum thinks the world of you."

The ferry took me across Port Philip Bay to Queenscliff, from where I took the coast road southwards. Just inland from here is Winchelsea, a small town of no importance, except that it was here in 1859 that a man called Thomas Austin decided that having a few rabbits about the place to shoot in the evening would improve the quality of life. He imported twenty-four rabbits from England and released them into the bush. Now rabbits exist to do only two things, eat and reproduce - both of which they do with considerable enthusiasm. Australia, having been isolated from the rest of the world for millions of years, didn't have a single predator that recognised a rabbit as part of the food chain, so the rabbits lived happily ever after, and went forth and multiplied ...and multiplied...

And in twenty years of chomping on the local herbage, the entire state of Victoria had been picked clean, leaving little fodder for the sheep or cattle. The rabbits hopped into New South Wales, and South Australia, and beyond. And, like furry locusts, they devoured everything in their paths. In the 1950s, after almost a hundred years of devastation, myxomatosis was introduced from South America as the solution to the problem. Although only about one rabbit in every thousand survived, they were the ones with a natural resistance to the disease and re-established a population of rabbits for whom the disease was no longer a threat - and now there are millions of them again. It is one of the world's great ecological disasters - the result of the monumental folly of one man.

I wanted to be near the sea so I took the road south, the Great Ocean Road, one of Australia's most scenic routes. Lorne, a small holiday resort with a golden sandy bay nestling against a steep, wooded hill, was my destination. The hostel was a series of chalets clinging to the side of the hill, with well-tended gardens adorned by the presence of white cockatoos.

I had not made a reservation. The receptionist glanced at the list and said, "I've only got one bed available tonight, but I'm afraid it's in a mixed dormitory." She looked at me, arched her eyebrows, and asked, "Do you have any objection to sleeping with five girls?"

"I can handle that, no problem," I asserted, maintaining a straight face. Mixed-sex dorms are common in Australia. Nobody gives a hoot. You just pile in and go to sleep.

Arriving at the dorm, I introduced myself to the only girl present, a young teacher from Melbourne. On hearing that I had been head of a school, she started asking questions about managing difficult kids, as this had been a major problem in her school. Well, that was something I knew a bit about. Throughout my career I seemed to have developed a reputation for handling difficult delinquents: somehow, I seemed able to establish a rapport with potential perverts, psychopaths, robbers, rapists and arsonists. Her interest was intense. We started talking at 4 p.m., and three hours later she interrupted me and said, "I'm getting hungry. Would you like to join me for dinner?" I don't often get invitations to dine with a young lady, so I joined her. We were still talking at 1:30 a.m.

She joined me for breakfast, during which she invited me to take a trip into the forest with her to view a spectacular waterfall a few miles away, and again we talked about education. I was planning a lengthy drive that day so, with some reluctance, we parted company after lunch.

"This has been fantastic," she said. "I have learned more from you in a few hours than I have in four years in teaching. I'd love to have worked with you, John."

That gave me a nice wee glow. She passed me a piece of paper with her address and telephone number on it. "If your are ever in Melbourne, give me a call."

Then she hugged me, and I glowed some more.

Chapter 23

THE ART OF SEDUCTION – AUSSIE STYLE

The weather in Victoria is like British weather – changeable. The temperature was a blistering 32°C when I left Lorne. Two hours later it had dropped to a shivery 18. I stopped to view the Twelve Apostles - a magnificent series of sea stacks strung out along a stretch of coast, lofty pinnacles and towering blocks of rock left stranded as the sea eroded the cliffs behind. The sky had clouded over, a chilly wind blew in from the sea, and the coastal vegetation looked remarkably similar to the scrub and heather of the north of Scotland. It would have been beautiful a few hours earlier - now it was bleak. It was hard to believe I was not back in Scotland.

This unforgiving stretch of coast is littered with 1200 shipwrecks, many of which had been packed with immigrants. There was a sense of poignancy that, after having endured the privation of six months or more at sea in the confined space of a sailing ship, the hopes and lives of hundreds of men, women and children were wrecked within a few miles of its destination. The sea, pounding against precipitous cliffs, offered little chance of survival on this inhospitable coast. Yet it has an awesome beauty.

The Twelve Apostles, Great Ocean Road, Victoria, Australia.

A few miles further on, I picked up a couple of hitchhiking backpackers. They had just alighted from another car as the rain came on. This was too much like Scottish weather to leave them standing. The boy was a hairy Englishman with a pair of bongo drums, his girlfriend an attractive French Canadian. She was a music student who was about to return to Quebec to pursue her studies. The boy intended to keep drifting on around Australia. They had been sleeping in a tent, and although interesting company, they smelt a bit musky. I dropped them on the outskirts of Port Fairy, opened the car windows - despite the chill - and headed into town to find the hostel.

A quaint little place with a lovely harbour, it is described as an historic town (although the description 'historic' is applied to anything over about 70 years old in Australia). With its timbered shops with balconies covering the sidewalks, it had more of a frontier town appearance than I'd seen anywhere else. Take away the cars and you could be living in the last century. I liked it.

The following day, I turned inland to explore the Grampian Mountains - being a Scot, I could hardly ignore a place with a name like that! And there were many other Scottish place names along my route. I drove through Hamilton, along the Glenelg Highway, and passed through Dunkeld. It was like being back home. The Grampians, a cluster of rocky mountains with wooded slopes, offered a refreshing change from the miles of gentle rolling farm land, and I broke my journey to view one its tourist attractions, signposted, Scenic Waterfall.

After limping along a rocky trail through the forest for 20 minutes, I came upon a sheer rock face, bone dry save for a slight oozing of moisture among some green slime up at the top. A dripping tap would produce more water, and what oozed over the top had evaporated long before it reached the bottom - in fact, long before it had even left the top. The riverbed below the 'waterfall' was a sun-baked jumble of rocks, with not a trace of moisture anywhere.

I felt conned, and hobbled back through the forest to the car park, passing other suckers with cameras intent on photographing this mighty cataract. I never told them they were wasting their time. Let them find out for themselves. I had passed plenty on my way in, and not one had told me there was not a drop of water to be seen. Besides, the walk would do them good.

Hall's Gap is a snug village in a narrow, steep-sided valley with a distinctly Alpine feel to it. After dinner at the local hostel, most of the residents retired to the TV room to watch the film, *Lord of The Rings*. Never having been an enthusiast for the works of Tolkein, I settled quietly in the common room to read. Some girls arrived: a couple of Aussies and a bouncy Maori, and sat chatting opposite me. The Maori girl left, but breezed in a few moments later and announced that a lady in her dorm, who had been touring the wineries, was bringing down some wine. So too, were the two German girls in the dorm. Their plan was to have a 'Girls' Night.' I looked up from my book, coughed ostentatiously, and said, "I take it that's my hint to leave."

The Maori girl clasped her hands over her cheeks in horror. "Oh no! I didn't mean to be so rude. You must stay."

"Och no, if you're planning an all-girls night it would be quite improper of me to stay and spoil it for you." I stood up to leave. She blocked my exit, her eyes pleading.

"No. Please. You're making me feel terrible." And I was enjoying it too! I played up a bit more.

"No, no, no, I couldn't stay where I'm not wanted. I'll just take my book, and go and sit on my bed in the dormitory - alone."

"Oh, no! Please. Please. We want you to stay and join the party, don't we girls?" There was a chorus of approval. She pressed on. "Get him a drink, Lisa."

A glass of wine was thrust into my hand and Lisa joined forces against me. Both girls now had their hands on me forcing me back into my seat. Well, not wanting to spill the wine and with my leg still not in good shape, I lacked the power to resist their efforts and, with a feigned display of reluctance, I agreed to stay. Just to make them feel better, you understand! To assuage their guilt they lavished attention on me, keeping my glass full, and chatting with me. What had started as a quiet, solitary evening was turning out to be very sociable indeed - and it became livelier still.

Lisa had found some music, turned up the stereo, and the dancing began. Despite my protests, I was hauled to my feet. They outnumbered me six to one, so I had little chance of repelling their advances. It would have been impolite of me not to perform my gentlemanly duty so I put aside personal considerations and allowed my hips to sway to the rhythm of the music. I had no rest for the remainder of the evening. A few other guys came as far as the door, but hadn't the courage to join in. The manager looked in, reminded Donnalee, the Maori girl, of the curfew on noise at 11 p.m., shook his head in disbelief, and retreated to his office. We boogied on till the quiet hour, and the girls began to drift off. I gathered the glasses and took them to the kitchen to wash up.

Lisa joined me, and we chatted comfortably. In the space of the few minutes it took to wash seven glasses the conversation changed from being superficial to something more personal.

"I'm really glad you stayed, John," she told me, "it made the evening so much more fun."

"Och, I fair enjoyed myself," I remarked, laying the last glass on the drainer.

"You're a very unusual man." She picked the glass up and dried it.

"In what way?" I dried my hands, leaned back against the work surface, and regarded her with interest. She was an attractive, vivacious girl, dark haired, probably of Mediterranean descent.

She laughed lightly. "You're not what I would have expected of a retired headmaster. You have such a sense of fun, and to go backpacking round the world and do all the things you've done, especially after having lost your wife… not many people would do that."

"Well, I look on retirement not as old age, but as my second youth."

"That's a great attitude." She hung the tea towel on a rail to dry and confronted me. "Have you never considered re-marrying?"

"No."

"Any relationships since your wife died?"

"No."

"Why not?"

I shrugged. "I'm not against the idea, but I find it difficult to imagine myself in another relationship. I haven't been out looking for one - and a queue hasn't exactly been forming at my door."

"You should think about it, John. Don't close your mind to it. I think you are ready for a relationship now."

"I keep an open mind, but to be honest, at my age it isn't likely."

"How old are you? If you don't mind me asking?"

"Sixty-one."

She tilted her head and smiled. "You look much younger."

"Flatterer."

"No. I mean it. And you have a young attitude to life."

"Aye…I suppose mixing with young people all my life has helped, and travelling gives me the opportunity to enjoy the company of bright, young people. That's one of the things I like about it."

"Why are you travelling, John?"

"Several reasons, I suppose. I enjoy meeting people, experiencing different cultures, trying new activities like scuba diving."

"Are you running away from something?"

"I hadn't thought of it like that." I chuckled. "Maybe from the miserable Scottish weather! I don't mind being alone, but sometimes your thoughts get ambushed and then you feel the pain of loneliness. This is much more fun and no more expensive."

"I think you are running away from something, John."

"Oh? What?"

"I think you are running away from a relationship - or at least the possibility of one. You don't seem to me to be the kind of person who wants to be alone for the rest of his life; you're too sociable for that. You mix so well, and obviously like people. Maybe you're afraid of getting hurt again if it didn't last, but I think you should consider sharing your life with someone. You have a lot to offer." This was becoming provocative and I decided to change the focus. It was my turn now to ask the questions.

"Hey, you're not a psychologist are you? What do you do?"

"I'm a sales manager."

"Ah, a career girl?"

"Yes so far, but it's time I found a soul-mate."

"You don't have anyone then?"

"No. I've had three relationships in the past ten years, but none of them worked out - and now time is running out for me."

"How old are you?"

"Thirty-four." She looked at least ten years younger, and I told her so. "Thanks, but it's beginning to worry me. I need to find that special person before it all passes me by."

"I would have thought your chances were pretty good."

She shrugged. "Maybe, but I'm still looking for the right guy. What are you looking for John?"

"I'm– " The kitchen door flew open and Donnalee burst in.

"Oh, you've done all the washing up! Good. I just came to say goodnight. I'm going to bed now. Thank you for being such a good sport, John. It was a great party." She threw her arms around me and bid me goodnight. Then she turned to Lisa, "Right, coming up to the dorm then?"

Lisa flicked a hesitant glance at me. "Hmm, yes, I suppose so." She paused for a moment to hug me. "Thanks John. Meeting you was something special. Goodnight."

That night, I lay in bed and pondered. What had stimulated such an interest in my reasons for travel? How did she come to the conclusion I was running from the prospect of a relationship? I couldn't recall anything I had said that was of any significance, or that should stimulate such an interest, but it had happened, and all so quickly. Yet again, there had been the assertion that I should be sharing my life with someone - so it wasn't peculiar to the Fijians. Was I giving out subliminal messages? And what would have happened if Donnalee had not returned? This was all too much of a female thing. Relationships rarely feature in men's talk. Thoroughly bamboozled by it all, I drifted into sleep. I had to leave early in the morning. I didn't see the girls again.

Cecily, who had been following my itinerary with interest and apparently had friends all over Australia, had suggested by email that I should try to visit Berry Bridge Vineyard. One of the partners in the business, Iain MacDonald, was an old friend of hers. It sounded like a pleasant diversion, and as it was within a couple of hours drive, I headed north again. This was deep in the heart of rural Victoria, an area of farms and vineyards baking in the sun. Virtually every river was dry, the grass a dull ochre; it was a landscape parched after weeks of drought. There were few towns, and the roads off the main highway were gravel.

Iain was away in Tasmania. Rod, his partner, on hearing that I had come all the way from Scotland, insisted that I stay awhile.

"I can't let you go back to Scotland without giving you a cup of tea," he said, as though it were just a couple of hours drive away. I seldom refuse a cup of tea, so we sat on the veranda and talked. By mid-day I reckoned I should be on my way, but again he wouldn't let me go. "No, no. You're staying for some lunch. I'm enjoying the company."

He prepared a delicious salad lunch and opened a bottle of the vineyard's own Shiraz. As I was driving I only took one glass. We sat on the veranda talking for another couple of hours before I had to drag myself away to continue my travels

- and Rod had to drag himself away to pretend he was doing some work. I doubted that he would do much: he had supped my share of the wine.

I asked if I could buy a couple of bottles of his wine to take to Graeme and Helen.

He looked at me pityingly: "John, you're only a bloody backpacker, mate. You can't afford to spend money on this kind of wine. This is a small vineyard aiming at the quality end of the market. This stuff sells at $32 a bottle! No. Just go into a liquor store and buy a couple of $5 bottles to take to your friends."

I laughed and took no offence. I loved the outspoken bluntness of the Aussies. I fired a salvo back. "Maybe I am only a backpacker, but I'm not your average Antipodean, impecunious, scruff. I am a gentleman backpacker, who appreciates fine wine - and generous hospitality - and these friends of mine deserve the best. Besides, if this drought continues, you're going to need every dollar you can get - so get off your arse and open up your cellar!"

He raised his eyebrows, shrugged, and capitulated. I had enjoyed my visit to Berry Bridge very much. Cecily had dealt an ace card again.

In the morning I took the road back to Warragul. Helen was having some friends over for 'a bit of a barbie' that night and, having brought some quality Berry Bridge wine, I was allowed to join them.

As it happened, the girls were all drinking vodka, so Graeme and I were left with the onerous task of consuming the wine. Guys don't often share confidences as girls do, but there comes a point, usually somewhere near the end of the second bottle, when their heads lean closer together, they become very matey, and begin to talk from the heart. I therefore found myself responding to Graeme's curiosity about what I got up to on my travels through Victoria. He listened intently, and when I described my conversation with Lisa he shook his head sadly, put his arm round my shoulder, and said with that depth of feeling that only the inebriated are capable of, "You need help, mate."

"Eh? Why?"

"You need to learn how to close a deal."

"What are you talking about? What deal?"

"John, I've only known you for a few days, but I can see you're a fair dinkum sort of bloke. You're a good conversationalist, very sociable - in fact damned good company - and I can understand why Helen was so thrilled to see you again. Your coming here meant a lot to her, and to be perfectly frank about it, for an old guy you're…. Well… You're actually quite presentable."

I had to laugh.

"No, seriously John, I mean it. No one would ever guess you're sixty-one. You hardly look a day over…. sixty! But look at it this way. You're a bright, intelligent bloke, yet you've wandered across the Pacific islands and squandered any number of chances with all these women in Fiji. Here, you've had two nice Aussie girls lusting after you, yet you've failed every time to close the deal. You did all the groundwork, but you didn't get it all together in the end. Get my meaning?"

"But we were only having interesting conversations." I protested.

"Bollocks! They were panting after you, and you didn't even notice! Now John, I know you're a product of a different culture, a different age even, when you had to court a girl for at least three years and put a wedding ring on her finger before you could climb into bed with her, but you're in Australia now, in the 21st century. We do things differently here. Stimulating, intellectual conversation is all very well, but there comes a time when you've got to break the flow and say, 'This is all very interesting, but are we spending the rest of the night at your place or mine?' That's what I mean about closing the deal."

Maybe he's right. Maybe I am thick, but I dismissed the idea that I could ever adopt the courtship rituals of *Homo Sapiens Australis*, the dominant characteristic of which seemed to be a distinct lack of subtlety or sophistication. You'll find polar bears in the outback before you'll find any trace of subtlety or sophistication in the Australian male when he's on heat.

"What happened to the art of wooing? And in any case," I argued, "how could I possibly invite a lady to share a night of passion with me in a backpackers' dormitory with five or six other people listening in - and if they were Aussies, more likely cheering us on?"

He looked at me sagely, and said quietly. "Find a nice secluded spot outside and put a blanket on the ground."

I shook my head in disbelief. "What? In a country crawling with poisonous snakes and spiders, all prowling about looking for a meal in the hours of darkness? Anyway, I don't have a blanket."

Helen's parents, who had also settled in Australia, insisted that I visit them on my way through New South Wales. I was to take the car again, leave it with them, and take the bus on from there to Sydney. While I packed in the morning, Graeme busied himself with checking the car. I tossed my pack into the boot and gave Helen a farewell hug, then shook hands with Graeme.

"All systems checked and in working order," he announced and opened the door for me. "By the way," he pointed to a travel blanket folded neatly on the back seat. "Just in case you get lucky."

"Aye, that'll be the day," I growled.

And in case you're wondering - I never did get the chance to use it.

Chapter 24

MORE REUNIONS

D O NOT BRING FRUIT INTO NEW SOUTH WALES proclaimed a large roadside sign. I had a banana with me so I pulled over and ate it. These Aussies seem to be all big guys, and I saw no point in upsetting them. As I munched on my banana I read the small print on the sign. It seems that fruit flies are the problem. They can leave eggs undetected on fruit and when the flies emerge they can inflict colossal damage on the fruit crop. Fruit flies are not all the same, apparently, and incomer flies may well be immune to sprays used to control the local flies.

They are very fussy about such things in Australia, and failure to declare any foodstuffs on entering the country can lead to hefty fines. Even the soles of your feet are examined at the airports for traces of soil or any other organic matter which might harbour organisms. Harsh lessons have been learned about interfering with the balance of nature - they haven't forgotten about the rabbits.

Another sign, which I ignored, proclaimed the good news to all northbound travellers that the next McDonald's fast food restaurant was only 126 kilometres ahead! Isn't that clever marketing? Imagine Ma, Pa and the kids driving along the highway. "Yippee! Don't forget to stop, Dad. Are we nearly there yet, dad? How far to go now, Dad?" That sign ensures that for the next hour and a half the children's digestive juices will be flowing, and father's resistance is going to be eroded away. But a Big Mac does nothing for my digestive juices.

The forests around the state border gave way to rolling hills and farmland, and I turned off the highway to seek out Helen's parents who lived in a small village. I had now driven over two thousand miles in Australia, but where were all the kangaroos? Dead at the roadside appeared to be the answer. At night they are a hazard to motorists - and themselves. The road verges were sprinkled with carnage from the night before. In ten weeks in Australia I only saw one live kangaroo in the bush (come to think of it, I never saw a single rabbit!), but I saw plenty of dead kangaroos.

Rural New South Wales was quite attractive. It is dotted with pleasant coastal towns and sleepy villages filled with second hand bookshops and antique shops. As with 'historic' buildings, 'antique' is a relative term. Seeing three antique shops in one village, all within a few yards of each other, I had to stop to see what they were selling. One or two items may have been as much as a hundred years old, but most of the stuff was familiar to me as the kind of crockery, furniture, and brassware in common use in my youth. I didn't need to be reminded that *I* was an antiquity, so I moved on.

The other kind of shop that appeared in every village sold what I would call New Age trinkets: wind chimes, tinkling bells, strange star-shaped decorations, candles, incense burners, hookahs, magic carpets… that kind of thing. Eastern mysticism seemed to be in fashion. Signs advertising land for sale - Lifestyle Plots - were everywhere.

'Escape the rat race, become a 'Lifestyler' and live the quiet life in the country with your cats, wind chimes, and the smell of incense; wear hippie clothes, and cultivate a few cannabis plants in some quiet corner of the woods…Live the Australian dream,' was the impression it gave me. The economics of it puzzled me: I couldn't fathom how they made a living selling junk antiques, second hand books, and trinkets to one another. But just about everything about Australia defies understanding. It is a fascinating country.

After enjoying a couple of days of excellent hospitality with Helen's parents, I took the bus to Sydney. It was an eight-hour trip, the early part of which was illuminated by the monologue of an intellectually challenged young lady who was acquainted with the driver, and kept up an incessant commentary on events of stupefying inconsequence.

"What d'ya have for breakfast, Roy? I had scrambled eggs and toast, Roy. Mmm, scrummmy they were, Roy. I'm going to see my cousins today, Roy. Two girls and a guy, Roy. They'll all be at the bus stop to meet me, Roy. How's that for a welcoming party, Roy? Not one, but three of them, Roy. I'm such an important person, it takes three people to meet me, Roy. These horses are still in that field, Roy. They're at it again, Roy. They were at it last time I was here, Roy. Did you see them, Roy? They're always at it, Roy. They spit at you if you go near them, Roy. They spat at me last time I went up there, Roy."

This went on incessantly for two hours. I closed my eyes and tried to shut it all out by going to sleep. Who ever heard of a horse spitting at you? But maybe she was right. This was Australia, after all. When I woke up she was gone.

Sydney harbour is magnificent. Quite apart from its two icons, the Opera House and the Sydney Harbour Bridge, it has one of the world's great natural harbours, allowing large ships to come right into the city centre. It bustles with life: ferries, freighters, cruise liners, harbour tugs, and yachts are constantly on the move, creating a dynamic pastiche of colour, style, and ceaseless energy. It is the kind of place where you can sit all day and gaze and never get bored. People of every nationality throng its streets. It is a brash, vulgar, and, at times, elegant city. Sydney is typically Australian.

Here, I did feel a sense of history, albeit fairly recent. Just over a century ago the clipper ship, *Cutty Sark,* tied up at its wharves to load wool, and then made some of the fastest passages ever logged by a sailing ship as it crossed the Southern Ocean and round Cape Horn, to bring the wool to Britain. Just to the south of the city lies Botany Bay, reputed to be Captain Cook's landfall.

The company in the Central Youth Hostel in Sydney was a bit more entertaining than at Melbourne. At breakfast, I met a couple of elderly Americans from Seattle. Both in their seventies, they asked if they could join me at my table. They introduced themselves, and included me in their conversations. Jack, an enthusiastic traveller, was lean, mean, and athletic looking. Bob was portly, of more homely appearance, and remarkably similar in looks, voice, and mannerisms to that genial former Hollywood film star, James Stewart. Bob was not enthusiastic at all about travelling outside the USA.

"I allowed this guy to talk me into coming to Australia for six weeks," he growled in his slow drawl (here was another graduate of the American School of Slow Talking). He shook his head slowly. Everything he did was done slowly. "Biggest mistake of my life. Too hot. And too many flies. I hate the place. Can't wait to get home."

Although close friends for many years, they fell out over almost everything. During the flight out, they argued so much they couldn't bear the sight of each other, and Bob asked the flight attendant if he could move to a vacant seat about as far as possible from Jack. They met for breakfast and dinner, but went sightseeing separately each day.

"It's the only way I can stop myself from killing him," muttered Bob.

Back home they both owned RVs - recreational vehicles, for the uninitiated. These large articulated motor homes are as big as an average house in the UK, and have extending sides to make them even bigger for overnight stops. These two old-timers always set off together for a bit of fishing and shooting in the mountains along the Canadian border. Despite the enormous size of the RVs, they each had to take their own to keep the peace. Jack always took the lead as Bob was such a slow driver.

"John, he drives so slow, grass grows in his tyre treads," Jack informed me. "We gotta plan on takin' a whole week for a weekend fishing trip. I tell you John, this guy's so slow, no one knows for sure if he's still alive. When he dies no one will notice the difference!"

Bob bristled at the insult and frothed at the mouth as he tried to spit the words out with some venom. "L-l-l-listen h-h-here," he spluttered, pointing his finger at Jack like a revolver. "Y-y-you wait! N-n-next time we're heading up north, I'll show ya. I'll come at ya so fast, I'll suck ya up the intake, chew ya up into little pieces, and spit ya out the exhaust!"

Jack shook his head and laughed.

"It ain't possible. He carries so much stuff in his RV he can never get it to go more'n thirty. He has so much stuff packed in there, he has to sleep on the sofa in the lounge 'cuz he cain't get into the bedroom. It's like a warehouse in there, piled high to the ceiling."

Bob laughed. He had to admit that he was a hoarder. "I jest like to make sure I have everything I'm gonna need, John."

"Everything you're gonna need?" howled Jack, "Y'ain't needin' any o' that stuff. Y'aint never used it yet!"

"But I might one day!" Bob roared back. Jack shook his head as Bob explained to me, "I like to take a few things with me, John - jest a few things to make life more comfortable. Y'see, I hitch up the RV to the truck. I gotta take my motorcycle, so I have a derrick fitted so I can hoist the motorcycle up on to the back of the truck. I got a boat on a trailer, and I hitch that to the back of the RV. And I got a canoe that sits inside the RV…."

"This guy takes more gear with him than the US Army - and that's only for a weekend fishing trip," screamed Jack. "And his house is the same. He pays $500 a month to hire a warehouse to store all the things he can't get in the house. He keeps buyin' - but he jest won't throw anything away."

"Aw, shut up!" snapped Bob and changed the subject. "Where're you goin' today?"

"The zoo," snapped Jack.

"Good. I hope they feed you to the lions! I'm goin' out to Bondi Beach, so I won't have to suffer lookin' at you. Lots of pretty bodies there, John." He gave me a wink with a twinkling eye. "What about you, John? Where're you headed for today?

"I'm taking the train out to Pendle Bay, about sixty miles north of here, to meet up with a former pupil."

"Hey, that's cool! Have a nice day." And they meant it. I loved them.

Andrew met me at the station and recognised me, even though 20 years had passed since I had taught him. He now managed a team of statisticians, analysing trial data for a multi-national pharmaceuticals corporation. One of my most able pupils, he had been a friend of my son, so we had much to talk about. We spent hours sitting on his balcony overlooking a beautiful bay, sipping cool beer, watching the surfers.

It was illuminating to hear the things he remembered as we reminisced. Much of what you say as a teacher simply trips off the tongue. It may be inconsequential to the teacher, but just a few choice words scattered, like seed, can have a significant effect on the students, influencing career decisions, and perhaps laying the foundations of a lifetime's work. It was a revelation to listen to his articulate observations on my teaching style, and how I had influenced him and many of his peers. The knowledge that a simple remark can have such a profound effect on the lives of others is a wee bit scary, but it's true - it was how I was inspired to enter the profession by my own mathematics teacher.

The following day, as he drove me to the airport at Sydney, we encountered one of the many bush fires that had been sweeping through New South Wales in the previous few days. We were lucky: the wind was blowing the flames and smoke away from the highway.

As my flight rose above Sydney, the sky to the west was obliterated by smoke. Four hundred homes were consumed that day by the blaze as it spread into the suburbs of Canberra. Thousands of hectares of bush had been scorched; yet although the trees are blackened, they survive the fires, and in a few weeks new growth will appear on their charred branches.

Australia is full of surprises.

Chapter 25

HOME BREW AND HAIRY LEGS

Queensland is my favourite of all the Australian states. It has a fantastic climate, glorious beaches, and lush forests with more different species of tree per hectare than you'll find in the entire North American continent and Europe put together. At least that's what the Queenslanders tell you. There is a downside to all this: it is populated by some of the most venomous and voracious animals on earth.

Funnel Web Spider.

Before I left home my younger son gave me a book entitled, *Healthy Travel in Australia*. Maybe it was a plan to get me to change my mind, for it was not comforting bedtime reading. The word '*Healthy*' in the title should be replaced by '*DON'T*.' Australia is home to more things that will bite, eat, or sting you to an agonising death than anywhere else in the entire world. It has the most venomous of just about everything, including the world's ten most deadly snakes. If they don't get you, the funnel web spider, the blue-ringed octopus, the paralysis tick, the stonefish, or the box jellyfish are all waiting their turn. They are the most lethal of their kind in the world - and Queensland has the greatest concentration of most of these in Australia.

Blue-Ringed Octopus

The golden rule is: Don't Touch Anything! Australia has furry caterpillars that can knock you out with a nibble. A type of cone shell with a venomous proboscis will go for you if you disturb it. Imagine!... Where else in the world could you be attacked by a sea shell? An estimated 100,000 crocodiles are lying in wait for silly tourists to offer themselves for lunch - and, would you believe it, some of them do.

But don't let that put you off; it is a marvellous place to visit. You simply need to exercise a little common sense, a commodity sometimes lacking among tourists.

Cairns, its most northerly city, is the gateway to the Great Barrier Reef and, as a diver, exploring the reef was my primary mission. I also hoped to meet Cecily sometime before journeying back to Brisbane. She lived some distance from Cairns, but had arranged for her parents, Bruce and Shirley, to meet me at the airport and look after me for a day or two before I went to sea. They lived in a valley a few miles inland from Cairns and helped with their son Nick's bush-trekking on horseback business, preparing lunches, and transporting clients to and from Cairns. I hadn't seen Bruce and Shirley for thirty-one years when Bruce, then a major in the Australian army, was attached to a British regiment in Germany. They welcomed me with great warmth, and with a lot of catching up to do, Bruce and I spent many relaxing hours sitting on the veranda, sipping his ice-cold, home-brewed beer.

This relaxing atmosphere was conducive to the telling of stories, and the two of us sat and entertained each other with long, convoluted tales, as old men do. When Bruce launched into a tale, ever considerate of my limited knowledge pertaining to military matters, he had to provide me with essential background information in order to set the story within a context that I could understand. That was very helpful, and really quite interesting for me. Maybe it was the effect of the home brew, but I had the vague impression that some of the stories were hijacked along the way, meaning we never actually got to the end of them. Somewhere in the telling, their beginnings had been lost, and Bruce had wandered off in a different direction, but that was of little consequence. We were quite happy to ramble on.

Shirley came to join us once she had the dinner in the oven and could relax for a few minutes, but she lacked the advantage of having swilled a glass or two of Bruce's potent beer down her throat and was struggling, in her pitiable state of sobriety, to make sense of what we were saying. There is only so much a sober and sensible woman can tolerate, and after a few minutes wallowing in confusion, she had to reach out and touch Bruce on the arm, in a most considerate way, and say, "Bru darlin', would you hurry up and get to the point!"

Startled by her interruption, Bruce looked at me blankly. "Yes. Umm… Er… what was I talking about, John?"

But I had no more idea than he had. It was all so familiar - I was just as guilty - but Shirley was far too much of a lady to interrupt my own tortuous tales. Or if she did, I was too inebriated to notice. And before I forget what the point of *this* story is, the point is that I enjoyed Bruce's stories very much. They were full of interesting and illuminating references to his distinguished military service, from which he retired with the rank of colonel.

Nick joined us for dinner and invited me to accompany a party of tourists on a trek into the bush next day. I had only been on horseback once before and felt a trifle uneasy. I didn't trust horses. And this was tropical rainforest in North Queensland, with the possibility of encountering so many things that might spook the horses, causing them to eject the rider. I had no desire to provide an easy meal for a snake, crocodile, or spider. But Nick dismissed my concerns. The rivers up here were quite safe, he assured me. The crocodiles inhabit the estuaries, and snakes will clear off when they hear the disturbance before they get trampled under horses' hooves. I needn't worry about them dangling from trees, waiting to snap at passers-by either. Nick would take the lead so they could bite him first, and any spiders' webs would be swept aside by him. That made me feel better. Australians delight in telling you the most horrific tales of all the creatures that will eat you or sting you to death - and then dismiss it as nothing to worry about. They overdose on machismo here. Anyway, in my quest for further adventures, I agreed to go.

My mount was a pleasant looking cuddy called O'Malley. I patted his nose, looked him straight in the eye, and told him who was the boss in this partnership, radiating my 'I'm the Headmaster' aura. He looked me straight in the eye for a moment. He knew I meant business and nodded his head in agreement. That was that sorted out. Okay, maybe he was just clearing away the flies, but it gave me a feeling of reassurance: I'm sure he understood. He did look quite intelligent, more so than many of the delinquents I'd had to deal with in my teaching career. I mounted him, but as soon as he moved I realised just what a mistake I had made.

Everyone was wearing jeans - well, everyone except me. I had been wearing shorts for months now, and it never occurred to me to dress differently for riding on horseback. But a horse has four legs, all moving independently of each other. With everything in contradictory motion, your legs rub against the saddle - and, believe me, bare skin wears out quicker than cowhide. The stirrup straps slid back and forward against the saddle and clamped on to the hairs on my legs, uprooting them painfully (the hairs - not the legs!). This is a cruel method of defoliation. Although they pull out only a few hairs at a time, they catch and tug at all the others to ensure that you will continue to suffer over a long period. By the end of the trek my inner legs had become raw, pink, flesh sensitive to any touch - like sunburn. But, dour Scot that I was, I endured the pain in silence. I hate admitting my stupidity!

Apart from that, it was a relaxing excursion through the forest. I loved the bit where we went splashing along a riverbed for a short distance. I had seen the cowboys do this in western films, and before long I was talking to O'Malley in a John Wayne style drawl. The horse seemed to understand it too. We got on just fine together. After a short break by the riverside we made our way back for Shirley's delicious salad lunch, washed down with Bruce's home brew.

Nick's 12 year-old daughter had been staying with Cecily, and she brought her home the following day. After a gap of thirty-one years, we met at last. Cecily had been an outstanding pupil. Now a woman in her mid-forties, she still had the same mental acuity and mischievous sense of fun.

Three very pleasurable hours drifted away as we sat on the veranda and talked until she had to leave for home.

As I waved her off, I marvelled at the power of the internet that had enabled me to be re-united, in Australia, 12,000 miles from home, with three of my most memorable pupils. It gave me a nice wee glow again - which more than matched the glow on my hairless legs.

Chapter 26

THE GREAT BARRIER REEF

Cairns, Queensland

airns is a mecca for backpackers. Crammed with hostels, dive shops, and tour operators, it offers exploration of the rainforests, white water rafting, kayaking, diving, snorkelling, and sailing. Everything is made easy for the visitor here. The hostels all offer advice on where to go, what to do, and they will arrange bookings, often with discounts, for all the excursions available. The streets are lined with inexpensive restaurants where you can sit and watch the adventure-seeking youth of the world stroll by, but the main attraction for me was the Great Barrier Reef.

Great Barrier Reef

A World Heritage Site, this incredible series of coral reefs extends for some 1250 miles along the east coast of Queensland. Visible from space, it is the world's largest living thing, the habitat of billions of polyps which secrete a hard blend of calcium carbonate and protein to form the coral that provides them with an external skeleton for support and habitation. Successive generations build on the skeletal remains of the old, and the coral has developed into rock-like formations. Over three thousand separate reefs and six hundred islands are home to more than fifteen hundred species of fish, and four thousand varieties of shellfish. The beauty and variety of its marine life is astonishing.

Diving opened up an amazing new world to be explored.

Glass-bottomed boats can offer a glimpse of what lies beneath the surface of the sea; snorkelling is fine in the shallower water, where many of the most colourful corals are to be found; but the reef can only be fully appreciated by diving. You can explore coral pinnacles, swim through dark tunnels and deep canyons lined with gently waving fronds of soft coral where you may encounter huge crayfish, large wrasse, malevolent looking moray eels, and perhaps a turtle having a leisurely feed. Fish of every size and shape, dressed in the most amazing colours, mingle in submarine coral cities. Here, the diver has the capability of flight, soaring at will, like a helicopter among skyscrapers, up and over the towering high-rise blocks of coral, or down among the traffic of yellow-streaked fish in the shadowy canyons between. You can glide along sunlit, sandy streets between coral formations pulsating with electrifying colours, feel the powerful thrust of water expelled by a giant clam snapping shut as you hover above its vice-like jaws, or swim in convoy with a turtle, imitating the graceful and effortless motion of its fins.

No matter how long you gaze, the childlike wonder grows. You inhabit a surreal world: alluring, mysterious, enchanting, populated by the most astonishing creatures; some beautiful, some bizarre in appearance. Yet all, in their infinite variety and dazzling colour, are supremely adapted for life in this silent, submarine world. The only sound is the rhythmic hiss and bubble of air passing through your regulator as you breathe, a reminder of the privilege bestowed upon you: that you are an alien in a world that defies the power of imagination to visualise. Far beyond anything you have ever witnessed before, it offers something akin to a spiritual experience: here, you have returned to the primordial ocean from which life on land emerged millions of years ago.

Encountering many strange and colourful animals

I had enrolled in a course to gain my Advanced Diver's Certificate. A three day course, it combined classroom work and study on board a specialist diving vessel out on the reef, with tuition on deep diving to 100 feet, night dives, underwater navigation by compass, underwater photography, and exploration. The dive boat offered excellent air-conditioned accommodation, plenty of good food, and all the necessary equipment.

Starting each day with a wake up call, we had to be in the water for a deep dive at 6 a.m. A pack of dark heads bobbing around in the water like seals, we released air from our buoyancy jackets and descended into the depths. Grouping together on the sandy bottom 100 feet below, we were asked to do some simple calculations on an underwater clipboard to demonstrate how the working of the mind is slowed at this depth by nitrogen narcosis. An egg was broken, yet the pressure of water around it kept it intact as we tossed it around the group like a rubber ball. A closed plastic bottle that had been taken down was crushed by the pressure. It was then filled with air, and when released, it shot up like a shell from a gun, the air expanding as pressure decreased until it exploded, a reminder of what can happen if you hold your breath as you ascend. Your concept of time diminishes and fifteen minutes at this depth seemed like only two or three - another important lesson.

Our slow ascent, slanting upwards along the coral wall, offered glimpses of its residents in the brightening daylight. As the sun rose higher in the sky it illuminated our world, like an artist at work, adding colour to a previously monochromatic backcloth. Shoals of fish darted, glinting silver, blue, green, red, and gold. Large wrasse with blunt noses glided silently past, quite unconcerned. Rays flapped their wings in elegant motion and soared upwards and away from us. Reef sharks prowled with lazy effortlessness, but kept their distance. Recumbent among the rocks lay the elegant spiral beauty of large triton shells. A startled octopus, its tentacles oozing over the rocks, withdrew shyly into a dark chamber. Giant clams with beautiful, intricately patterned, multicoloured membranes between their vice-like open jaws, shut tightly as we passed over them. No one complained about having to be roused so early. This was well worth getting out of bed for.

After breakfast, we were underwater again, practising navigation techniques. Around mid-day, while we were having lunch, the boat moved to another reef.

For night diving, we were supplied with waterproof torches, and descended into an eerie, gloomy world. When artificial light was shone upon the coral, it reflected colours that seemed to burn all the more brightly, like the embers of a glowing fire. As on land, the sea has its nocturnal creatures, species which were absent during the day. Sharks loomed silvery-grey out of the darkness, but darted away with a quick flick of the tail when a torch beam shone on them. The distant lights of other divers glowed mistily in the gloom, like car headlights in a fog.

Underwater photography presents challenges. Light is much less intense, so care must be taken to get reasonably close to the subject with the sun behind you when shooting pictures. I was so excited at the prospect of capturing vibrant images with my hired camera and started shooting pictures till Nick, one of my diving buddies, came across, took the camera from me, and turned it round. I had been taking close-up pictures of my own face! Our tutor added that to the course notes as one of the silly things *not* to do.

In three days we were kept busy with dives, lectures, and homework exercises, so there was relatively little time for socialising. We always dived in groups of two or more: your diving buddies look after you, you look after them, just in case anything goes wrong. Safety is paramount. You are always checked out and back on board again with the time, air pressure in your tanks, and length of rest periods between dives recorded. A few years previously, a couple were left behind at one reef. The crew had failed to notice their absence, and the boat returned to Cairns, about 30 miles away. It was two days later before anyone realised that they were missing. No trace of them has ever been found. Hollywood's interpretation of that story resulted in the film, *Open Water.*

My diving buddies were Nick, a 25 year-old Dane, and Jamie, a 21 year-old Canadian. During the three days afloat we became good friends - I would hate not to be on friendly terms with people on whom my life may depend. This action-packed, three days of living and learning in close proximity to other students had the flavour of life at university, where the work is intense and relationships develop quickly under pressure.

Table coral with blue-striped snappers.

All too soon it was over, but we were reluctant to sever the bonds of our new-found fellowship. We had established a dependence on one another in our undersea explorations, laughed, and teased our way through study and relaxation periods, opened up our lives in discussion as we relaxed on deck and at meal times, and the experience had left its mark on each of us.

On the way back to Cairns, we arranged to meet again at O'Brien's Irish Pub to celebrate our success: we were now Advanced Open Water Divers. Some of the others who had been on the boat joined us: a Dutch couple and a French couple, Els, a 21 year-old Belgian girl, and Ingrid, an 18 year-old Dutch girl. The two couples decided to have an early night, but the rest of us were in no hurry. Nick suggested we should go on to the Woolshed, a popular nightspot. Of course, I'm too old for that kind of thing, but Nick would have none of it and, as in Rarotonga, I was dragged along with them.

It was bedlam! The place was heaving, packed solid with bodies. Girls were dancing on the chairs, tables, anywhere there was a bit of surface to gyrate on. I could only stand and stare, lost in wonder. Jamie, Ingrid, and Els soon had enough of this, and had the sense to leave. But I was curious. I was interested in observing this strange form of social behaviour - from an intellectual standpoint, of course.

A cry disturbed my reverie: "John! How are you?" It was Jules and Sarah, two English girls who had also been on the dive boat, but had left a day earlier than us. After chatting for a few minutes - well, shouting at each other is more accurate as the music was so loud - Sarah leaned towards me to speak. I had to lean forward to hear what she was saying.

"I just love hearing you talk, John. Your Scottish accent is wonderful."

That took me aback. "Really? I always thought it was as common as muck."

She leaned forward again. I could feel her lips caressing the edge of my ears.

"Oh no! It is so attractive. Think of Sean Connery. Who could ever say he sounded common. I could listen to you all night."

Well, this was becoming interesting, I thought. I remembered Graeme's advice about closing a deal, and was about to offer her the chance to do just that when the music changed and Jules grabbed Sarah by the arm. "Come on, let's dance," she yelled, and hauled her into the press of bodies writhing on the dance floor. I stayed where I was. I hadn't been included in the invitation. In my day, men invited ladies to dance. Now they go it alone.

Besides, I didn't have a blanket to put on the ground.

The place was so tightly packed that it was virtually impossible to dance anyway. All I could do was stand there surrounded by girls, their writhing bodies rubbing against me. If I let my hands fall to my side, in front, or behind me, and turned my palms outward, it was inevitable that some pert little bottom would wiggle its way into my hands. It was so effortless. And nobody seemed to notice. I just stood there on one spot with my hands dangling, and without a hint of invitation - or even the slightest vestige of embarrassment - beautifully rounded female bottoms, oscillating to the rhythm of the music, thrust themselves on to my palms.

Sad, isn't it, what an old man has to do to get a thrill.

Now you don't really believe that, do you?

Chapter 27

DIAGNOSIS AND DISMAY

In the lingering euphoria that followed my certification as an Advanced Diver, I felt compelled to go diving again. I snapped up a great deal at almost half-price: a five-day diving trip on what was regarded as the best part of the Great Barrier Reef. However, talking to Nick and Jamie about it that night, they both urged me to see a doctor as my ankle was still swollen since the incident on Fiji. Then Rod, the hostel manager, who had been expressing some concern about it since I arrived in Cairns, looked at it in the morning and ordered me to get to a doctor at once. It had now been six weeks since the injury had occurred in Fiji and it was taking more time to heal than I expected.

I went to a doctor, who asked the usual embarrassing questions: "How did did this happen? And when?"

When he heard my tale, he shook his head and rolled his eyes, and sent me to have an ultrasound scan. Another doctor there looked at the picture and asked me how and when it had happened, and he too shook his head and rolled his eyes.

He told me: "The Achilles tendon is completely severed. There is a three centimetre gap between the ends, and if you don't have surgery soon the gap will widen further. It may then prove impossible to repair the damage, and you'll never be able to lift your heel again. Your calf muscle will become redundant and will deteriorate through lack of use, and you will be physically impaired for the rest of your life. You'll become a decrepit old man, a mere shadow of your former agile self, and you'll be scuppered for diving, and sailing, and dancing - or even standing holding your hands by your side, allowing pretty young ladies to press their pert little bottoms into them. You'll not even be able to get on to the dance floor because you'll be bloody-well crippled!"

Or words to that effect. Australian doctors do have a rather brusque bedside manner.

I was then despatched to see a surgeon, who also shook his head and rolled his eyes and - well, you know the story by now!

He said, "I can operate tomorrow, but you'll be cemented into a full-leg plaster cast for at least three weeks, then we'll change that to a lighter cast. You will be immobilised for at least three months before you can go home - the airlines will not accept you as a passenger with your leg in plaster. The operation will cost you $2100 - and that doesn't include the post operative consultations, or my fee for this consultation."

Maybe he detected a change in my colour when he mentioned the cost, for he then went on a different tack.

"Alternatively, you can wait up to six months to have it done under Australia's reciprocal health care arrangements with the

UK, but since your holiday is now completely buggered…" (His words not mine! As I said, they are quite brusque)… "why don't you just go home and have it done in Scotland for free, like all the other tight-fisted Scots gits?"

Or words to that effect. I reckoned he realised he was on a loser this time. I left to consult my insurers.

They would only support private treatment in an emergency, otherwise I had to be treated under the reciprocal health care agreement. Having tramped merrily around Australia for six weeks, gone horse riding, and completed 14 dives with a broken Achilles tendon rather spoiled my chances of being treated as an emergency. With only five weeks of my trip left, the most sensible course of action was to abort the trip, return to Scotland, and recuperate from surgery at home. So that was that. Forget going on to Bali. Go home.

Looking on the bright side, at least I wouldn't have to sit around a backpackers' hostel totally incapacitated for three months gnashing my teeth as I watched all the others go out to play, telling me what a wonderful day they'd had diving, rafting, kayaking, bungee jumping, or boogieing the night away at the Woolshed packed with pert little bottoms. Much better to be at home in chilly Scotland instead of lying about, sweating in the tropical sun, with bronzed young ladies all hovering around me, lavishing sympathy and care and attention on me, helping me to my feet and inviting me to put my arm over their shoulders while they clutched my body and helped me get to my dormitory to tuck me into bed at night - and feeling my leg to see it was getting any better…

With my strict Calvinistic upbringing, I was doomed to endure pain and suffering in order to remain virtuous and achieve eternal life, so there was no option but to abort the trip and go home. On hearing the news, Bruce and Shirley immediately offered to care for me, but three months of me with a leg in plaster, inactive and grumpy, was too much to inflict on anyone.

Of course, I suffered some disappointment, but you've got to trim your sails to suit the wind, so I booked flight for the following week.

My planned diving excursion had to be cancelled, but I could still fit in a short trip to Cape Tribulation, where Captain Cook's ship, *Endeavour*, had to be beached for repairs after being holed when it struck a reef. That area had other geographical features called Weary Bay, Mount Sorrow, Mount Dismay, Cape Disappointment, Cape Catastrophe - all very apt in my present circumstances. It was Cook who gave them these names. He was 12,000 miles from home with a big hole in his ship and he was forced to beach her up a creek for seven weeks for repairs with hordes of unfriendly aboriginals and hungry crocodiles milling around. He wasn't feeling too cheery either. Compared with his predicament, I couldn't really complain.

It was hard to be gloomy for long here. Our bus driver had a fund of entertaining stories about the horrors lurking around Cape Tribulation: "You guys can't fail to be impressed by all the lovely beaches we have here in Queensland. But just ask yourself one question: why are they all empty? Not a single swimmer in sight.

Box Jellyfish

"Well, the reason is this… October to May is the stinger season, when the beaches near to the river mouths and creeks are populated by box jellyfish, which breed in the estuaries. You don't want to go meddling with these little monsters. Even a dead one can sting you. Don't even think about going for a paddle along the shore. If you get stung you can count the seconds till you depart this life. And if you get beyond ninety you are not lucky - you are in hell! - because the pain is said to be beyond anything man can conceive. A year or two back, one young and very stupid backpacker ignored all the warnings - you can't miss them, warning signs are posted everywhere - and he went for a swim at the height of the stinger season. Within a couple of minutes he got stung, and started screaming in agony. His mates dragged him out of the water. His back looked liked he'd been whipped with barbed wire, and even though there were paramedics on the beach to administer first aid, he rapidly went comatose. They pumped enough morphine to kill a horse into him, yet he was still screaming blue murder even though unconscious. He died within a few minutes. That explains why, with all the beautiful beaches around, you don't see anyone swimming."

Daintree National Park

That shut us all up... But there was more to come.

Our route took us across the Daintree River by ferry. Large warning signs tell you that these are crocodile-infested waters - a cue for another story.

"Look at all these signs. You can't fail to get the message. Right?... Wrong! In spite of the fact that people make a good living from running boat trips along the river to let the tourists see the crocodiles, a group of tourists who'd had a bit of a party one night decided it would be fun to have a skinny dip in the river. A girl called Beryl - she was only up to her knees in water - bent down to skim the surface of the water with her hand when she suddenly disappeared. Taken by a crocodile!

Not even a scream was heard. She was found by a search party a couple of days later beside a large, well-fed crocodile. It was his last meal, for they shot him.

Stay clear of crocodiles.

"There are two lessons to be learned from this story. First, virtually every crocodile casualty is alcohol related - and it's not the bloody crocodile that's been drinking! It has only behaved as nature intended. Secondly, given a choice, a crocodile will always select the smallest person around as its prey. That's the easiest target, and the meat is usually more tender and easier to digest. The men in this instance had all been swimming in deeper water, and one guy even felt the crocodile brush against him as it made its attack run. So, guys, the moral of this story is: if you plan on swimming in crocodile infested water, take your girlfriend with you. The crocodile will always go for her first!"

I love the Australian sense of humour.

The Daintree Forest is another World Heritage Site. Plants have survived here that became extinct elsewhere in the world millions of years ago. It is a biological time warp, a dense steamy forest with trees covered in straggling creepers, populated by pythons which grow up to 10 metres long, and numerous other snakes, lizards, tree kangaroos, and cassowaries. The cassowary is a large emu type of bird with razor sharp claws that can kill a man - everything else does, so why not the cassowary too? There are large vociferous frogs that croak deafeningly through the night, millions of insects that chirrup in the trees so loudly it feels like you are in the middle of a huge sports stadium with screaming fans following your every movement, deadly spiders, and a stinging tree that won't kill you, but will make you wish it had. It is the kind of place in which you could easily visualise dinosaurs prowling - and you wouldn't be a bit surprised if you met one.

It is not difficult to get lost, our driver told us. "Another word of warning if you plan to go bush walking. People get lost here all the time." (Australia does seem to be remarkably adept at reducing the world's population!) "So if any of you plan on going walkabout, make sure you tell the people at the hostel. Fill out one of the safety forms with details of your route and when you expect to return, and leave it with them."

We all nodded obediently.

He went on, "Not that it'll do you much good. One guy went off a few years ago on what should have been a six-hour hike up Mount Sorrow. No one bothered to check the safety sheets, and even though he'd left his tent pitched in the grounds of a backpackers' hostel, it was three weeks later before they realised he was missing. He's never been seen since."

Despite the horror stories, there was still a vestige of adventure left in me and I went walking in the jungle (well, hobbling is more accurate, with my bad leg) with all these thoughts in my mind. I did not wander far. I stuck strictly to the sign-posted paths and boardwalks that had been laid across the swamps, and the fact that you are reading this now is proof that I am still alive after strolling casually in the company of all the horrors lurking there. I began to wonder if the driver had made it all up, for all I saw was one sluggish terrapin.

Back at the hostel, we were warned not to leave any food lying around in the kitchen because it encourages nocturnal visitors, such as snakes. The hostel didn't have windows, just holes in the wall to keep the place cool, which increased the likelihood of meeting a snake if you wandered into the kitchen for a drink of water in the dark. It wasn't too inviting outside either, with Golden Orb Spiders' webs, a metre in diameter, suspended between the eaves and the nearby trees. The spiders' bodies were as long and thick as my little finger, and their legs would have spanned my entire hand if laid on the palm, but they were beautiful, with golden rings circling each leg. They are said to be harmless. The forest comes alive at night with all sorts of rustlings in the undergrowth, bats fluttering around, toads and frogs belching at each other. The noise is amazing, but it wasn't the sort of place to go stumbling around in the dark, so I took a book to bed and had an early night.

In the morning, I set off sea-kayaking from a beautiful bay with soft white sand - and not a jellyfish in sight. It was a perfect day, with the surface of the sea like glass, allowing us to view the coral below, and observe turtles and rays swimming underneath us. Our guide led us round Cape Tribulation and we beached the boats for a picnic. He then took us for a short walk up a shallow creek among the mangroves to visit the resident crocodile. From about 50 metres away we watched it, motionless as a log. Had it not been for the guide pointing it out to us we could have wandered along blissfully unaware that it wasn't a log. This was not a place for the uninitiated to go stumbling around.

Not far from the hostel lived the bat-woman - a woman who walked around, festooned with bats clinging to her shirt. She ran a bat sanctuary and told us about the bats' lifestyle and the research programme currently being undertaken there. The bats were big, with bodies the size of a weasel and wings about 18 inches long. As she stroked and fondled them, they snuffled like young puppies. The wings were beautiful to touch; delicate, and smooth as silk. Bats, like tarantulas, sharks, and wolves, have been much maligned by ill-informed writers and Hollywood film makers in their quest for scaring people. These creatures were beautiful, cuddly, and appeared to be affectionate.

On my return to Cairns, I wanted to say farewell to my diving buddies and wandered out to see if I could find Jamie and Nick on my final night. O'Brien's Irish Pub was the most likely place to find them. On entering, I heard a cry, "John, John! Over here!" It was Els and Ingrid. "Come and join us."

I sat down at their table and gave them my news. On hearing that I was leaving in the morning, Ingrid immediately called up Jamie and Nick on her mobile phone. They arrived a few minutes later. They were all so sympathetic. We talked for a while and exchanged addresses, and I issued an invitation to them all to visit me in Scotland and come sailing with me.

I excused myself to go to the toilet. When I returned, Jamie and Nick both put their arms around my shoulders and said, "We've just been talking about you, John, and your fantastic lifestyle. You know, for such an *old* guy, you're really quite young at heart!" I felt another wee glow and it helped to ease the ache I felt I my heart. I hoped that I might be privileged to meet them all sometime in the future.

I left Cairns at 8 a.m. the next morning to fly to Singapore, then to London, and onward to Inverness, where my son and his wife met me to drive me home. Forty-two hours after leaving Cairns, I walked through the door of my house in Lochcarron.

Now I had to talk to my own doctor about my Achilles Tendon.

Chapter 28

ON THE MEND

I presented my doctor with the x-rays the Australian doctor had given me. He studied them and looked at me incredulously. "You walked in here with scarcely a limp and no sign of pain."

"I have the Fijian bush medicine to thank for that." I replied.

He examined my leg. "We must get you into hospital as soon as possible and have it repaired before there is any further deterioration in the calf muscle."

The surgeon was equally astonished. He asked me to walk across his consulting room. "I don't know how you can do that without feeling extreme pain," he said.

"Maybe the Fijians know something we don't," I said.

"Maybe… but bush medicine won't bring the two ends of your broken tendon back together. Only surgery can do that."

He then explained: "Your foot will be angled to draw the heel closer to the back of your leg to allow us to get the two ends of the Achilles Tendon as close together as possible. We will then join them with a steel clamp. It is important to keep your leg in this position to allow a join to form naturally, so your whole leg from hip to toes will be encased in a plaster cast.

After about four weeks we will remove the cast, and if all is well we will replace it with a cast from the toes to your knee. You will need to wear this shorter cast for another two months. We will provide you with crutches to allow you some mobility."

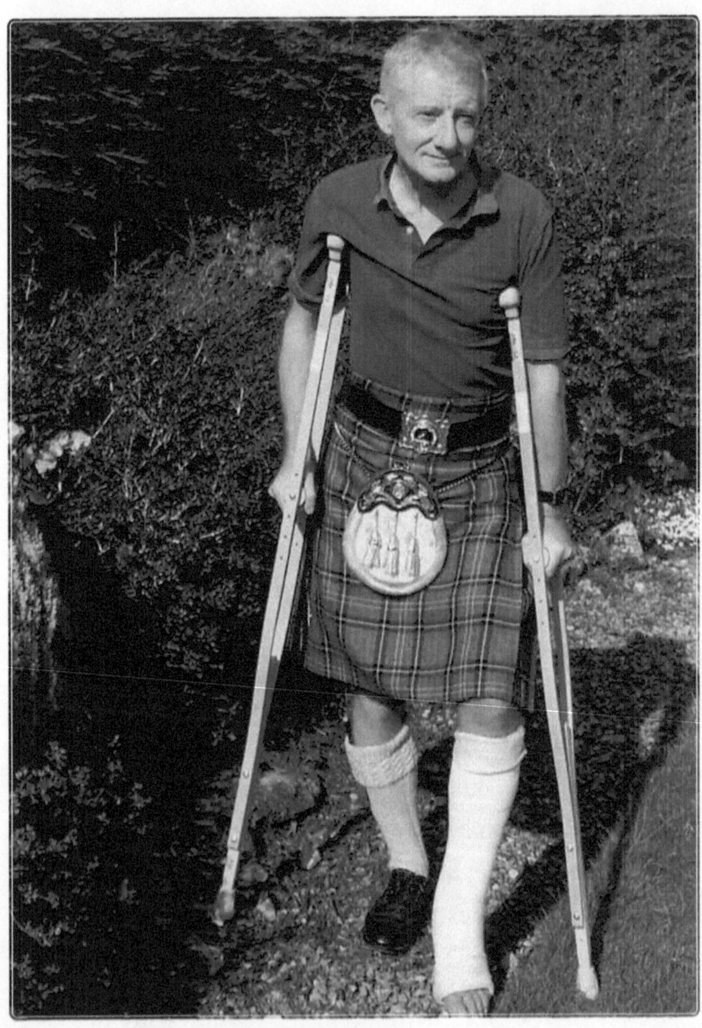

A kilt is easier to get into than trousers when
you have a plaster cast on the leg.

Amazingly, I suffered no pain after the operation. When I regained consciousness, I asked the nurse what the tube plugged into my arm was for. It was proving to be an irritation to me.

"That's your morphine pump. Just squeeze this button here with your finger and you'll get a shot to keep the pain under control."

"But I don't feel any pain."

"You will, when the effects of the anaesthetic finally wear off."

Late at night, when she came round doing her checks, she looked at the reading on the morphine pump. "You haven't taken any morphine," she scolded.

"I don't need any." I retorted. She drew me a pained look.

"You don't *have* to suffer, you know."

"But I'm *not* suffering. I don't need it. You might as well take all this damned plumbing out of my arm. It's just getting in a fankle when I turn round to sleep on my side."

"Of course you need it. You've just had major surgery. You've been cut open and had bits of you pinned together, and you've been sewn up again. You're bound to feel pain."

I rolled my eyes. She noticed.

"If you don't like taking morphine, I can give you some paracetamol tablets instead."

"What for?"

"For the pain!" She was getting exasperated with me.

"But-I-don't-have-any-pain!" I hammered the words out. I was getting exasperated with her. "Now will you kindly disconnect all the plumbing and let me get back to sleep."

She placed her hands on her hips and tilted her head. She didn't have to say anything. I could read the body language:

"Oh, I would love to give this one a right good slap." Aye, she's determined to get me to feel pain one way or another, I thought. We squared up to each other, and I glowered back. She could read my body language too. She knew she couldn't touch me, not with my leg in plaster from hip to toe, not just after an operation. I had the ace card. She cracked.

"I'll have to ask the doctor."

Five minutes later, she returned with a doctor. He asked me a few questions about the pain I was not feeling.

"Look," I swung my legs off the bed and grabbed my crutches. "I can walk without any pain." I almost galloped across the floor. "I'll dance the Highland Fling for you if you want. There is *no* pain!"

'Okay. Stop. That won't be necessary. You've proved your point. Disconnect the tube, nurse."

I had been warned by the doctor to take things easy for at least a year – and no single-handed sailing that summer! That was a major blow, but if I had to be beached I might as well turn the enforced convalescence to some advantage. With my leg in full length plaster I started writing this book. It took several more years to complete, but it gave me a purpose in life while my mobility was restricted.

I also spent some time working on a new design for my kitchen - it was in need of major surgery too. I started assembling units while still using crutches, but when the plaster came off my leg I got busy on the demolition work, with a few days invaluable help from my son, stripping everything back to the bare walls and rock underneath. The re-construction took up most of the summer, but in rest periods my mind was busy planning my next trip round the world.

I wanted to get back to Australia to take that live-aboard dive trip I'd had to cancel. I was determined to visit my friends who had cared for me so well in Fiji, and a return visit to the Cook Islands was also a priority. From there I could hop over to Easter Island, then onwards across the Pacific Ocean to Chile and Argentina to trek among the Patagonian Mountains. A voyage from Tierra del Fuego could take me across the stormy Drake Passage to Antarctica. And I could break my journey home and spend a few days with my nephew and his wife in Sao Paulo, Brazil.

Despite my infirmity, it had been a productive summer with mental activity more than compensating for my limited mobility. I recalled, 'Je pense, dunc je suis,' the words of the French lady I had met on the ship to Bora Bora, and my response in Latin, *Cogito ergo sum* - I think therefore I am. These words had guided me through my convalescence. As long as I could think, I could be creative, and I could plan for the future. Seven months after leaving Australia, I was on my way back, seeking adventure once more.

I had recaptured my youth.